MAKE ME BEHAVE

NANCY PIRRI

TARA FOX HALL

MAKE ME BEHAVE

First Printing: 2012

ISBN: 978-1-61235-479-8

Published by Satin Romance
An Imprint of Melange Books, LLC
White Bear Lake, MN 55110
www.satinromance.com

Published in the United States of America.

Cover Design by Caroline Andrus

MAKE ME BEHAVE

Feeling naughty? Included in this anthology are five stories of women looking for some 'kink' in their lives, and the men that willingly oblige them. These romantic stories are fun and sexy and include domestic discipline and spanking.

MANAGING MIRANDA

NANCY PIRRI

Miranda Russell is worried her husband is losing interest in her so she devises a plan to gain his attention. The fact is, her workaholic husband, Justin, has no idea he's not spending enough time with his lovely wife, until she surprises him at his company's holiday party, completely disobeying his order not to purchase a new gown.

MANAGING MIRANDA

Seattle
Present Day
The Marshall household

Justin Marshall yanked open the double doors of the closet and pointed inside. "Miranda, now tell me again that you've nothing to wear to the holiday ball."

Miranda sat on the edge of their bed in her prettiest nightie. The short baby-doll top was sheer and nude-colored, split from neck to waist and held together with tiny lace ties marching down the front, her bottom encased in a matching thong. The nightie left nothing to the imagination and Miranda had worn it with one solitary purpose in mind, enticing her husband into allowing her to purchase a new gown for his company's holiday ball.

Justin wasn't a cheap husband. On the contrary, he was exceedingly generous and rarely questioned her shopping trips, though for some unknown reason, this time he questioned plenty.

As she flicked her gaze over the rainbow myriad of gowns, then met his stubborn, narrow-eyed expression, she had the distinct feeling she wasn't going to win this argument. With his pointed glare, she imagined she could see fumes of fury lifting from his body, his anger completely focused on her. His brow was furrowed, his neck muscles tight, and he clenched his fists at his side.

Her handsome husband had reached his limit. That was a good thing. She wanted his attention—even if it was angry attention.

He slammed the doors shut and faced her, his hands settled low on his lean hips.

Miranda eyed his widespread long legs. She'd riled him but not to the point where he'd completely lose his patience with her. She came to her feet and gazed adoringly into his startling blue eyes. Reaching up, she settled her arms around his neck and brushed her breasts against his suit jacket, offering him a smile.

"You know I'd be satisfied to wear any one of those gowns, any other time, but your ball committee planned a theme and a particular color—red."

He reached up, pulled her arms from around his neck, and took them in a firm grasp. "You'll make do with what you have, and I don't want to hear another word about it." He released her and raked his fingers through his dark curly hair he wore short so there were no unruly curls to ruin his businessman's image. "It's bad enough I had to move my clothes to one of the spare bedroom closets. You must stop this obsession you have with clothes."

She pouted. "But I haven't a single red gown in that closet, honey."

He opened the door again and stuffed his hand among the dresses. "What about this one?" he said and pulled out a fist full of fabric.

"That's burgundy."

He shoved the fabric back inside, and then slammed the doors closed once more. "Red comes in several shades and that gown qualifies. You'll wear one of the gowns here or you won't attend the ball with me. I'll go alone."

"You can't go without me, Justin!" she protested as she sank to the bed again. Her lower lip trembled and her eyes filled with tears as she hugged herself. "How could you even think such a thing?"

"You give me no choice. You need to learn a lesson."

He started pacing the floor, his jaw set, a scowl on his face. His reaction to her tears surprised her. Usually, he'd take her in his arms, cuddle her, kiss her, and wipe away her tears, offering apologies. But her tears weren't making any impression on him this time. Then guilt seeped inside her and she bit her lip as a little voice deep inside chided her; she should be ashamed of herself. By having purchased too much clothing, the ever-growing wedge between them had widened.

In the past, by allowing him to have his way with her in the bedroom, she usually managed to get her way. Now she was faced with a perplexing problem;

he hadn't seemed interested in sex lately. As a matter of fact, he didn't seem much interested in her in any other way, either. Her heart stilled at the awful thought that he'd lost interest in her and tears flowed freely down her cheeks

Miranda's frustration had built to an all-time high. Having no sex for weeks on end just wasn't right—wasn't normal. Her heart raced now in anguish at the possibility he no longer loved her and her crying grew louder.

Last month, desperation had prompted her to order the *Super Vibrator* from an online sex toyshop. She didn't try and hide the toy from Justin, either, knowing he could easily stumble upon it if he opened her dresser drawer, in search of one of his own article of clothing she occasionally mixed in with hers. While the tool was powerful and gave her mind-blowing orgasms, it just wasn't the same as making love with her husband. Yet, she wished he'd found it. The man deserved to know he had a little competition.

She tilted up her chin and scowled at him. "Give me some of your time and attention and I'll be happy to stop the shopping trips!" she snapped. His only response was to pause in his pacing and raise his eyebrows at her. She sighed and added, "Can we talk about this a bit—"

He interrupted her. "I'm taking a shower and turning in. I need to be in the office by six. As far as I'm concerned, this discussion is over."

She cursed under her breath as she watched him amble into the adjoining bathroom and calmly shut the door. Typical. His calm was one of the things that had initially attracted her to him. Now all she wanted to do was throw a shoe at him.

Justin's calm was a stark contrast to her father who ranted and raved about every little thing. Justin's composure had inspired a feeling of trust and safety, and yet now she'd give anything to get a rise out of him.

It had been over a month since they'd made love, and she felt deprived, both physically and emotionally. While he'd always been the aggressor in their marriage, it seemed now, if she ever wanted him to make love to her again, she would need to be the one to make the first move, not that she hadn't been trying by leaving vivid hints which he ignored.

She hoped their life would soon return to normal. Justin would work his typical eight-hour day and come home to her, eat a delightful supper prepared by their cook, join her in a bubbly glass of champagne or two before tumbling into bed together and exhausting themselves in blazing hot sex. She was twelve years younger than Justin. Seven years ago, he'd pursued her with a gentle ferocity she'd never known from any other man. Consequently, she'd fallen madly in love and married him after a whirlwind three-month courtship. She sighed, thinking how things had changed. Once more—she'd try once more tonight.

She slid into the bed, under the covers, thinking about ways to spice up their lovemaking—things she'd read on the internet. Her interest had first been caught by stories that involved spanking. She had then moved onto watching spanking videos. It had been titillating reading the stories on those sites, and the pictures of women of all shapes and sizes getting their behinds walloped prompted shivers of delight up her spine. As she thought about those strong men disciplining their mates, she decided she would welcome even that kind of attention from Justin.

What if she could make him so angry he wouldn't be able to control himself as he usually did; what if she did something so naughty he'd have no recourse but to bend her over his knee, pull up her skirt (or pull down her pants) and spank her bottom until it was red and shiny as an apple? Her bottom clenched at the thought as she tried to think of a plan to become a thoroughly bratty wife. Pain mixed with pleasure suited her thoughts, for at least he'd be giving her some attention.

An idea came to her then; she'd purchase a new gown for the ball, to the tune of an exorbitant amount of money even her wealthy husband couldn't ignore. She sighed, knowing well their disagreement wasn't about the money she spent, but about his feeling that she shopped way too much, overfilling their closets. Then she thought over the 'theme' of the ball, 'Yesterday, Today, and Tomorrow' and decided *three* dresses were in order; one for yesterday, one for today, and one for tomorrow—the past, present, and future, all in red. She would divide up the evening and wear each gown accordingly.

Would this antic be the one to finally pull his chain, yank him right over the edge so he'd punish her as she'd been longing for him to do? God, she hoped so! Lord, she'd even smashed up his prized Lexus a few months ago, quite by accident, of course. He'd given her little more than a tongue-lashing, so great had been his anxiety and relief that she hadn't been harmed in the accident.

He came out of the bathroom, naked, the way he always slept. Her eyes glazed over as she gazed at his exquisite body, long, lean, and sinewy. He slid in beside her, reached for the remote that turned off the overhead fanlight, plunging the room into darkness.

Excitement soared through her when she felt him turn toward her—reach for her. He slid a hand across her abdomen, rubbed her bare skin in tiny circles and she turned to face him. Hope soared through her as she thought, finally! Miranda reached out and touched his chest but he pulled his hand away from her, pecked her on the forehead, and said, "Just saying good night, darling. Like I said, I've an early morning."

She heard him rustling with the sheet, felt the bed dip as he turned his back on her.

Tears filled her eyes. He'd rebuked and rebuffed her—again. Damn him. The tears slid down her cheeks as she stared up at the ceiling. Her heart ached at the thought that he was falling out of love with her. She shook her head, unable to believe it could be true; but other than being exhausted from working long days, what other reason could he have for ignoring her? Could he have another woman in his life? Could he even now be contemplating leaving her?

Stifling her piteous sniffles, she closed her eyes, reached up and swiped her cheeks with her palms.

A plan—she needed to flesh out *the* plan. As she thought over how to win him back again, she grinned at the thought of the large limit left on her credit card. He'd be furious, she decided, but prayed her plan would save their marriage. She loved Justin and hopefully, soon, he'd remember he loved her as well.

One week later

Miranda had spent two days searching for dresses. For the first hour of the ball, she planned on wearing a vintage-styled gown for 'yesterday'. For the second portion, she'd wear a sexy, slinky gown for 'today', and for the third she'd wear a dress of the future, which she had a difficult time envisioning.

She'd immediately found the dress for 'today'. It was a slim column of red satin covered with tiny matching beads that hugged her curves. It was strapless, and exquisite, even if it weighed a ton due to the beading.

She'd had no luck finding a dress portraying yesterday until the clerk in the last shop she'd entered advised her to visit an antique shop on Grand Avenue that carried vintage clothing. Now she stood in front of a full-length mirror in Granny's Attic, attired in a full-skirted gown over a stiff hoop, embellished with lace at the shoulders, neckline, and cuffs. She held a parasol over one shoulder and stared at her reflection, grinning from ear to ear.

"It's lovely on you, Mrs. Marshall," said the store clerk. "Would you like me to wrap it up?"

"The cost?"

"Oh, it's really a good buy at three-hundred."

Miranda gulped but said, "Yes. I must have this." She felt like Scarlet O'Hara in *Gone with the Wind* in the antebellum-styled gown.

She changed into her clothes and handed her charge card to the clerk. As she leaned over the counter and signed the receipt, she gulped again. Four-hundred for a gown she'd likely only wear once. But if it afforded her the results she believed it would, it was worth the price.

Upon reaching her recent model Honda™ she opened the trunk and tucked the gown inside with the first one she'd purchased; one curve hugging and sophisticated, the other full, frothy and utterly feminine.

For the remainder of the day she went from shop to shop but found not a single gown that would be perfect for the 'tomorrow' theme. An exasperated sales clerk at the mall asked her to be precise about what type of gown she was seeking. Miranda had no idea. The clerk shrugged and suggested a particular shop that might have something appropriate.

Soon Miranda found herself peering from her car's window at Thorns and Roses, a porn shop in a seedy part of town. Damning the clerk at the previous store, she looked around covertly as she exited her car and locked the door, then scuttled inside the shop. Moments later, she was delighted to find exactly what she had been looking for. But, was she daring enough to wear it?

The clerk who sported short spiky blue hair, tattoos all over her exposed flesh and a ring in her nose explained the gown's purpose; it was to be worn at a place where *scenes* were enacted—scenes of bondage and discipline.

"You're kidding, right?" Miranda said.

The girl smirked. "Don't worry. These scenes are private affairs. Hey, I think you'd look dynamite in it. Try it on."

Miranda was shocked when she did. No way could she wear this dress at the company ball, let alone stepping out of this dressing room.

She stared at her reflection in the mirror, stunned. The dress was made of red leather, hugged her body from shoulder to floor. From the front, the dress appeared sedate with its high neckline and long narrow sleeves. She blushed furiously when she turned and stared over her shoulder at the backside of the gown, or rather, the lack of it. Two straps held the dress in place; one crossed her middle back and the other at her waist, astonishment settling in at the view of her completely exposed ass. Below that wide-open expanse of flesh, the red leather was snug and molded to her thighs and down her legs.

Dismayed, she stared at her fully exposed ass cheeks separated just by her tiny thong and knew she couldn't wear it. She started to pull the dress off when the sales clerk said outside the dressing room door, "How about it? Like it?"

"Uh, I don't think it's quite 'me'," Miranda murmured.

"Let me see."

Before Miranda could stop the girl, she opened the door and smiled. "It's meant to be worn without underwear so once you ditch the thong it'll be perfect. You look fantastic in it. How about if you wear it with one of the detachable panels that attaches at the back? It's for more inhibited folks, like you," she said, grinning.

When the girl produced a long train of red satin and hitched it cleverly to the band at the waist and upper thighs, it trailed along the floor and concealed her attributes, except if she took too long a stride.

Miranda admitted, after a thorough perusal, she looked hot in the leather and purchased it, all the while thinking about Justin's reaction once he saw her in the gown.

She'd arrived home well before Justin so she had time to call Casey Bennett, her best friend, who also happened to be the caterer for the event.

"Casey? I've a favor to ask…"

The evening of the ball

November 17 had arrived. Miranda left the bedroom attired in the old burgundy gown and found Justin waiting for her at the foot of the stairs in the front hallway. Her heart raced at his appreciative gaze and she almost put aside the ridiculous idea of wearing the gowns she'd purchased—almost. When she reached him, he tucked her into an exquisite black velvet cape he'd purchased for her last winter. Winding an arm around her waist he pulled her against his side and escorted her to the limousine—Justin's only means of travel to special events—driver in attendance

"There, now, you look beautiful in that gown, sweetheart," he murmured, leaning down and brushing her lips with his.

"Thanks," she said demurely, knowing she did indeed appear beautiful. Her eyes swept over him. He was so handsome in his midnight-colored tuxedo she couldn't keep her eyes off him, which was nothing new. He always affected her that way.

He was being so kind, and solicitous of her, she almost regretting having the bought the dresses. Bu then she knew, this was one night; tomorrow he would be right back to his busy, workaholic life, and ignoring her.

They arrived at the Imperial Ballroom and, as they entered the high-ceilinged, spacious room, Miranda gasped in delight. Swaths of red and gold chiffon draped across the ceiling, embellished with glimmering white lights. The décor was exquisite. Casey had done her best work.

Miranda planned her strategy as she walked beside her husband. The women guests had made choices in their attire, most of them wearing gowns set in the present. A few wore vintage-style gowns, and none it seemed from the future, which prompted her to think about her own daring gown. Now she wasn't sure she could pull off wearing it.

She decided, before it was time to be seated for dinner, she'd change into her 'yesterday' gown. She sent a covert glance around, noted Justin talking with one of his employees before slipping from the ballroom.

Casey had picked up Miranda's gowns the day before and promised to store them in the coat checkroom. She retrieved the old-fashioned gown first and changed in the Lady's room. Once she exited, parasol in hand, she sauntered back to the ballroom and ran smack into her husband. She'd hoped to avoid him for a while, believing she had the perfect opportunity since she'd be sitting on the opposite end of the table from him. But no, he was right there, an astonished expression on his face that quickly changed to irritation.

Justin grabbed her elbow and escorted her into the ballroom. Between gritted teeth, he seethed, "Where in the hell did that dress come from?"

"Just a little something I picked up last week."

He rolled his eyes. "Didn't I say no to a new dress? You spent a fortune on new clothes just three months ago. As it stands now, I have to have more closets built to accommodate *your* wardrobe."

"Now that's a wonderful idea! Why didn't we think of that sooner?"

"Stop it right now," he snapped as he settled her into her seat, which was, indeed, on the opposite end of the table from him. "We'll talk about this when we get home," he promised, then left her and took his own seat.

Chills traveled up Miranda's spine. She'd caught the look in her husband's eyes and guessed that he hadn't finished with her yet. *Wonderful!* She was more than ready to go toe to toe with him.

The gentleman beside her, who looked remarkably like Paul Newman, though his name was John Smith, held her attention with delightful conversation. It seemed the man had traveled the world and she found she was enthralled by his vivid tales.

She rarely traveled because Justin never seemed to manage to secure any time off work. Oh, how she'd love to take a cruise with him, or even simply sit on a beach in Jamaica for a week. Or secure a job. But that was out of the question; she'd worked as Justin's secretary and, once he'd proposed, he'd insisted she quit working and concentrate on making a home for them.

He'd encouraged her to return to school, however, and earn her college degree. She'd graduated just a few months ago with a degree in business. He had immediately offered her a job in his company but she decided against working for him. Seeing him twenty-four-seven was not a good idea so she started concentrating on redecorating and updating their home. He'd been delighted with the changes. Then, when he brought up the idea of having a baby soon she couldn't have been happier. She slumped, depression settling in. She knew she wouldn't be conceiving a baby any time soon since they didn't have intercourse often enough.

Now, as she sat at the table chatting with the man on her right, she raised her champagne glass to her lips as her gaze settled on her husband's face where he sat at the opposite end of the table. Anger boiled beneath his calm veneer— she could see it in his eyes. She raised her glass and swallowed down the contents. Her husband's nostrils flared, even from the vast distance, she noted with a gulp. Thankfully, he remained in his chair and wouldn't cause a scene. Oh, a scene was what she wanted all right, but in the privacy of their home. Tilting up her chin, she kept her gaze leveled on him then he turned away with a disgusted look.

Miranda sniffed. So much for making him jealous, she mused in disappointment. He was furious with her, and she guessed soon, with the changing of the next gown, she suspected she would push him over the edge…

She smiled, her sadness disappearing at the thought of having him then, right where she wanted.

After dinner, she left the table, pausing to pick up the next gown from the coat check. She changed into the next dress and left the Lady's room just as her husband approached. His eyes glinted in steely anger. "Dance with me," he ordered.

"Delighted," she said and he swept her into his arms.

Justin held her close, slow dancing, his left hand smoothing the fabric of the red beaded gown against her back. She gasped when he daringly swept his hand lower, then he cupped her ass cheeks and pulled her up against his hard body; precisely against a mighty erection she hadn't felt in a long time.

"Another gown?" His eyes gleamed, smoldering with desire. Her eyes widened with anticipation, unable to recall when she'd last seen *that* look in his eyes.

"Of course," she said, "this one's for the 'today' theme."

He leaned close and his breath fanning her ear when he spoke, sent shivers up her spine. "Tomorrow, you will take both dresses back to the store."

She pulled out of his arms. "They won't take them back now that I've worn them."

"You will try, at the very least, and if the shops won't allow you to return them, I'm afraid you'll be very, very sorry." He scrutinized her and softly added, "You've never really seen me angry, have you?"

Miranda gulped and shook her head, thinking, *show me, though, damn it, after seven years of marriage! Show me some heat, some spark, some kink!*

"You don't want to see that side of me. You really don't," he warned.

Oh, yes, I do! Her heart thumped wildly in her chest as she stared into his hardened face. Never had she seen his eyes so cold, so unforgiving. She almost felt as though she'd never known him, so foreign did he appear wearing this severe expression.

She thought back to her high school tennis coach, who'd had his own manner of disciplining his charges; she'd been on the receiving end of Mr. Foster's fraternity-style paddle on several occasions when he felt her performance less than adequate. Private schools ran them the way they wanted, and this school believed in each teacher's decision to use corporal punishment or not.

Her senior year was the last time she'd received any form of corporal discipline and her ass tingled at the thought of feeling the smack of well-polished hard wood against her buttocks once more; feeling the sting of it as pain radiated over every inch of both cheeks, up her spine and down her legs. The coach had forewarned all of the girls and their parents of his training method. Miranda and her parents had willingly signed on, even with his unorthodox methods. She'd turned out to be a damned fine tennis player because of the discipline. Miranda could only hope to provoke Justin into treating her in a similar fashion.

Her cheeks flushed when she saw people staring at them. He noticed, too, and took her in his arms again and danced until the music stopped. Then he slid his hand to her waist and escorted her from the floor. She squealed in surprise when he smacked his palm against her ass just as she bent to take her seat. She shot straight up and heard him say behind her, "Just a little taste of what will happen tomorrow if you don't succeed in returning the gowns."

Miranda took her seat and a few gulps of warm champagne, grimacing. Glancing surreptitiously around her, she breathed a sigh of relief. No one had seen him smack her—or people chose not to let on that they had! She would have been humiliated and yet, another moment of excitement flared through her at the thought of others seeing him take her in hand.

Hope soared through her at his reaction, anxious for the evening to end. She looked at him as he stood in a circle, talking with some of his employees. When he made eye contact with her she saw a sexy glint in his blue eyes—one she hadn't seen in a long time—the one that had attracted her the moment she met him. Was it possible her plan was working? Hope and giddiness filtered through her body at the thought that it might be.

Marissa danced several dances with men she knew.

The dance would end at midnight, which was only an hour away so she scurried to the coat check to fetch her dress of the 'future'. In the ladies' room, she slipped it on, cringed and bit her lip worriedly. Damn, did she have the courage to wear it? Looking in a full-length mirror, turning side to side, she took an experimental few steps and gasped when the length of her thighs and glimpses of her ass showed. Her heart raced as she thought about Justin's reaction. Again, she gulped, and then daringly left the Lady's room, but taking smaller steps.

Was it her imagination or were people staring at her more than they had before? She turned as a man passed by, and she found his gaze settled on her ass. Not her imagination at all.

After dropping off the contemporary dress in the coatcheck, she paused in the doorway to the ballroom, her hands clenching as she looked for Justin. Disappointed he wasn't nearby, she stepped into the room and hugged a wall, until a man she later learned was the date of one of her husband's software engineers, approached her.

Miranda regretted accepting his request to dance shortly after the music started. His hand had settled initially at her waist but within a nano-second, he slid it down lower, until part of his hand was on her ass. She met his gaze and she saw he was drunk and leering at her.

"Excuse me," she said sweetly, but take your hand off my ass."

His leer grew. "Why? I like it fine right there, sweetheart."

Pressing against his chest with both hands, she gave a mighty shove. He stumbled back and released her but returned immediately, pressing his hand right in the center of her ass cheeks. Shoving against his chest a second time didn't work and she shrieked when his searching hand found the part where the panel joined the rest of her dress and he slid his hand inside and squeezed one naked cheek.

He gave her a wolfish grin. "Well, well, what have we here?"

"Stop it!" She pulled his hand off her. His hand came right back, slapping against her ass. Fury built inside her. The only one she wanted smacking her ass was Justin. When she tried pulling out of his arms, he wound his own around her tighter, keeping her in an unwanted embrace.

"Let's find a private place. I want to do a bit more exploring," he murmured. Then he bit her earlobe hard enough that she screamed in fury. Miranda stomped down on his foot with her stiletto heel.

She got the results she wanted for he immediately released her.

"You bitch!" he growled. "Who in the hell do you think you are?"

"The boss's wife," she said haughtily.

"Apologize to my wife."

The cold voice of her husband behind her made her release her breath in relief.

"I'll be goddamned if I—"

Her husband hauled back a fist and punched the man in the nose, effectively ending his profanities. Blood gushed from him and he landed on the floor, flat on his back...out cold.

Miranda was stunned. Never had she seen such anger from her husband.

Justin turned a disgusted look on Miranda as he took her arm and hustled her from the ballroom. At the coat check, he grabbed her long velvet cape and draped it around her shoulders, tying the ribbons. "Where are the dresses?" he snapped.

"Here, in the coatcheck," she whispered, and sniffled simultaneously.

He went into the room once more, found the gowns, and tossed them over his shoulder, grabbing her arm in passing as he headed for the door leading outside.

Guests swarmed into the hallway and Justin paused, Miranda at his side, and sent a scowl at them. "Continue, enjoy yourselves. My wife and I have just learned of urgent business at home."

He strode away, dragging Miranda with him. He ignored all of the questions being shot at them.

"Justin? Are you mad at me?"

"Yes, I believe I've reached my saturation point."

"Please, let me explain."

"Sure, we have all night for you to explain. And all night for you to sing, too."

"What?" she asked confused.

As he ushered her into the limousine and got in beside her, he said, "You know, singing, as in bellowing at the top of your lungs when I beat your sassy ass red for behaving like such a brat. For behavior which is completely unlike you, and unwarranted."

Slowly she nodded as her dark yet exciting future loomed ahead of her. A mixture of fear of the unknown and anticipation made her shiver. The limousine pulled away from the curb. Heat stoked Miranda's cheeks when she caught the driver's gaze in the rear-view mirror. Damn, she had a feeling the man had heard Justin's remarks.

Miranda settled gingerly against the back of the seat, her hands clenched in her lap as she waited for her husband to make a move. She sent him a covert look. His jaw was set, his lips thinned, eyes glinting in anger. Perhaps she'd pushed him too far. He didn't utter a single word and she didn't dare start a conversation. She sat quietly, waiting for him to say something...do something.

They arrived home. Justin helped her out of the limousine and she scurried ahead of him, to their lovingly restored Victorian home with an open front porch, surrounded by a white painted railing. She knew she was in a heap of trouble since he hadn't uttered a word in the limo. Then she slowed down. Wait a minute? Wasn't that what she wanted? Some kind of physical reaction from him? As she strolled ahead of him, her spine tingled as she heard his steps gaining on her. Just as she reached the front door, he took her arm and stopped her. It took all of her might to conceal the growing smile on her lips at the same moment the motion detection light came on.

"Bend over," he ordered.

Miranda gave him a confused look. "What in the world—"

He pressed down on her back, forcing her to bend over the waist-high railing.

"Justin!" Suddenly unsure, yet excited and fascinated, she looked at him over one shoulder, following his gaze. Miranda gasped at how the light shone down on her ass still covered in red satin. "What are you doing?"

He held her body down with one hand in the center of her back. "I want to see what you're wearing that caused that man to assault you. Now hold still." He slid his hand from one smooth, satin-clad shoulder to the buttons at the waistline of her dress where the panel was fastened. His nimble fingers found the six tiny buttons across the back and the four on each side and he released the panel. Miranda felt the fabric slide down her calves and pool around her ankles as a cool, early winter breeze caressed her ass.

Ohmygod, it was going to happen. Her husband was going to fuck her right on the front stoop where all their neighbors and passersby would see. Ripples of excitement tore through her body at the thought of being watched by others. She remained in position, waiting for him to begin, silently begging him to! She didn't care if the world saw them on her porch; she only cared she'd gained his rapt attention.

"Well, what have we here?" he asked, his voice soft as a feather's touch.

She started to straighten but he pressed her down again. "Stay put my dear, young, foolish wife. You've lots of explaining to do once we're inside, but for now, I'm going to avail myself of what that man was after."

Miranda's eyes widened in shock as he 'handled' her, for that was the appropriate word; no other word could explain the intimacy of his touch and the utter humiliation as he squeezed each of her butt cheeks. Oh! This was what she craved from him—had for so long, wasn't it? She could hardly believe it was happening.

She gasped when he slid one hand between her thighs and touched her clit. She groaned, putting all of her sexually frustrated feelings into that sound. When he slid a finger from her clit up to her anus, she stiffened and jammed her knees together in an effort to thwart his efforts. Back door antics had never been part of their lovemaking, even though he'd casually mentioned it a few times in the past. She'd fervently declined.

"Widen your legs, spread your feet apart," he ordered.

"Can't we please go inside, Justin?" she begged.

"Soon. Now tell me, where on God's green earth did you ever find such an ugly, albeit interesting dress?"

"Please, Justin, I don't want the neighbors to see us!" she begged.

"Not until I'm done inspecting the goods."

Goods? The rush of exquisite sensations diminished at his crassness. She was appalled at his words, shot straight up, and gave him a hard shove. Beneath the porch light, she saw his face darken at the same moment he reached for her again. Miranda gasped when he wound an arm around her waist, planted his foot on the lower rung of the railing, and then raised her up and draped her over his knee.

His big hand slapped her ass and she gasped again. Then satisfaction tore through her when she realized he was actually going to give her what she'd been afraid to say—a good hard spanking!

He pelted her ass with a very hard hand, alternating cheek to cheek, her gasps turned to groans.

"Not so hard, darling," she murmured.

He reprimanded her. "Get used to it. You've a lesson to learn, and it begins now."

Miranda cringed with each slap, yet a deep, warm feeling of contentment seeped into her body, both emotional and physical. Her ass tingled and she loved it! She imagined her buttocks had turned the color of beets since it felt hot, stinging, and had created a throbbing, delightful sensation between her thighs.

She felt wonderful! Yet she wondered if she'd done the right thing to drive him to disciplining her? Her conscience plagued her for she knew when he was through, he'd feel guilty. Afterwards, she would reassure him that she'd behaved badly to get his attention, and then he wouldn't feel so guilty. She soon changed her mind when his paddling grew harder, fiercer. "Ouch," she whispered.

"Ouch, sweetheart?" he drawled. "I've only just started."

"Not so hard." She moaned when he continued pelting her, not showing any sign of easing up, yet thankfully, not smacking her harder. His cadence was even and he kept his anger in check as he taught her a well-deserved lesson—one she'd been asking for!

"You are not the one in control, I am. I've had enough of your childish behavior. You will behave, as a good wife should. Why I didn't take you over my knee years ago when you misbehaved I've no idea, but from now on things will be different in our household, Miranda. Got it?"

"Yes, Justin," she said, compliantly, though that didn't stop him from pelting her ass.

Her bottom was truly stinging, as though she'd been stung by a nest of rampaging bees. Once again, second thoughts entered her mind. Damn. She heard herself moaning—couldn't prevent it. Squirming over his knee to avoid more smacks only made him hold onto her tighter. As pain increased, her moans did as well and soon she muffled her protests against his arm. There was nothing she wanted more now than to escape his hold.

"Enough, Justin! Stop now!" she begged again.

"Are you shedding tears yet?"

"No," she said but commenced sniffling.

"Good."

Good? What in the hell did he mean by that? He expected her to cry. And then she did cry. Like a leaky, faucet the tears started slow as she sobbed softly into the night. Tears of sadness she had felt over the past several months bubbled up until her sobs grew louder.

Now, feeling sorry for herself, for Justin, and the problems in their marriage, she wondered if they would ever have the love they first had seven years ago?

His paddling slowed a bit and she kicked her legs harder. He was too strong—too big—and she couldn't break his hold on her. Her dreams of erotic punishment were slowly vanishing in the face of this blatant, harsh reality. He'd started out with light, gentle strokes that had filled her heart and soul with joy, but his warm up hadn't gone on long enough, for almost immediately his slaps had changed to sharp, stinging punishment, though she admitted her coach's punishment had been more severe in comparison.

He paused, his open hand settling on her hot, stinging ass, as if he were gauging the heat. "Where did you purchase this dress?"

She sniffed, wondered if she should tell a little white lie, until his big hand smacked her again and she yelped. "At a shop called Thorns and Roses," she blurted.

"And its location?"

She clenched her buttocks knowing her answer would not make him happy. "On the south side," she hesitantly admitted. She'd barely told him when he started in again. He smacked her over and over again, on her sit spot until she shrieked, "Oh, shit!"

"Swearing, too? You know how I feel about that kind of language. And didn't I warn you about the dangers of the south side of town?"

"Ow! Ow! Ow! Justin, oh please, I won't go there ever again! And I won't swear ever again, but please stop," she wailed.

Abruptly, he did stop, pulled her up, and turned her to face him. "Sure you will. We're going to return all three dresses tomorrow. Perhaps, at Thorns and Roses, I'll find something to use on your ass instead of my hand!" He held his wrist limply. "Damn, I think I sprained it."

Miranda sniffed, leaned down to look at it. "If you did, I'm sorry." Again, her eyes welled with tears. "I didn't mean for this to happen."

He raised his brow. "What? You mean to tell me you *accidentally* purchased the dresses. Didn't I warn you, no more shopping?"

"Of course it wasn't accidental." She sighed. Reaching up, she placed her hands against his cheeks, pulling him down to her lips. He wound his arms around her waist, pulled her tight against him and her heart soared with joy when he kissed her—slanting his lips in one direction, then the other, his lips tantalizing hers. She stiffened in his arms when he started massaging her ass with one hand.

"Sore?" he murmured against her lips.

Miranda pulled back in his arms, releasing his lips. "An understatement if I ever heard one," she said, hearing the chagrin in her voice. Tears threatened again. She sniffled to hold them back. She felt happy, excited, and awful at the same time as that old guilt reared its ugly head.

"Why'd you do it, honey?" he asked.

Slumping against him, she whispered in a piteous voice, "All I wanted was some attention from you, that's all."

He raised his brow in obvious surprise. "Attention? You mean to tell me you *wanted* me to beat you?"

She swiped the tears from her cheeks and loosened her hair. It fell down her back and she smiled when she saw him suck in his breath. He'd always loved her wavy, golden hair and it had been a long time since he'd commented on it, or touched it.

"No, not a beating, just a bit of…" She shrugged. "Kinky sex."

He glanced around the yard then turned her around and pushed her ahead of him. "Inside—now."

She tripped into the foyer ahead of him. He slammed the door, flicked on the antique crystal light dangling overhead and tossed the red satin panel over a hook on the wall. Jamming his hands on his hips he said, "I'm listening."

Miranda turned around and saw the confusion on his face. She'd always loved his body. He wasn't too tall, around six feet, and he weighed in at a lean but muscular one-seventy-five. Damn, his body always seemed to be a distraction. Maybe it was because she hadn't gotten enough of him lately.

"You have no idea what I'm talking about, do you?"

"I'm no mind reader," he snapped.

She sniffed, felt self-conscious at the idea of confessing her deepest desires but she knew she must tell him how she felt. How she wanted him to spank her, tie her up and even play slave to his master, followed by some earth-shattering lovemaking. But embarrassment and feeling insecure admitting these feelings with him made her pause. She turned, took a step away and said, "I can't tell you."

Justin latched onto her wrist and dragged her around to face him. Scowling, he said, "Can't?" he asked, "or won't?"

"Both," she said as tears slid down her cheeks.

He groaned as he reached out and stroked one cheek. "None of that now. You've brought all of this on yourself, you know. "Now, unless you want another harsh lesson over my knee tell me the truth."

Miranda scowled at him. How could this man be so dense? Did she have to tell him outright? Couldn't he guess? She threw her hands up in exasperation.

"All right! I *wanted* you to spank me. Okay?" She rubbed her ass, pouting, and added, "But not quite so hard."

Justin stood there with an uncomprehending look on his face. He opened his mouth, closed it, frowning. He continued to stare at her.

"Oh, please say something! It's difficult enough for me to explain my feelings about this."

He gave her a narrow-eyed look. "How long have you been planning this?"

"For a long time. I just wasn't daring enough to do it until now."

"Is it…" he faltered a moment then gathered himself and said, "Is it because I don't satisfy you any longer? Is that it?"

"No! It's... it's that we rarely have sex anymore. I miss snuggling beside you, being held in your arms. I miss the funny little talks we used to have afterwards, talks about our lives together, our plans, and our dreams. Have you any idea, with all of your absences, how lonely I've been?" She took his hands, careful of the one he'd spanked her with. "I was afraid you were losing interest in me." She'd whispered the last, even as once again, tears slid down her cheeks.

His eyes widened and he pulled his hands from her grasp and wound them around her waist, pulling her close. "My God," he said, his words muffled in her hair, "What did I ever do to make you think that? You're dead wrong."

She pulled out of his embrace and turned her back on him. After a long moment's silence, she swiveled toward him once more and said, "When's the last time we made love, Justin?"

Justin sputtered as he raked a shaky hand through his hair. "Why, it was only.... well, maybe it was—" He sighed. "Guess I don't remember."

Her voice pleaded with him, "See, that isn't normal. I mean, you should want me as much as I want you. And believe me, I'm not telling you anything you don't already know but we won't have a baby if we don't have sex!"

"Yes, well, I don't see you crawling all over me to get any," he growled irritably.

"Damn, don't you blame this on me!"

Justin turned away and started pacing the floor. Miranda breathed a sigh of relief. Justin's pacing was a good sign. When he paced he went into deep thinking mode. He stopped in front of her and said softly, "Go on."

"You've rebuffed my advances the last few times I tried so I stopped trying. It's you and that damned business," she choked. "It's tearing us apart."

J ustin watched the tears slide down Miranda's cheeks and noticed the way she wrapped her arms around her chest, as if she found it necessary to hold herself together and thought that he must be the biggest jerk that ever lived. How could he have ignored her all this time? How could he have let his business become so important that he would ignore his beautiful, loving wife? Why hadn't he realized something was wrong? Why hadn't he seen they were drifting apart? He saw now. She'd opened his eyes to the fact. He couldn't lose her. He wouldn't. She loved him, and he loved her. And that's all that mattered.

However, if he wanted to save his marriage, he'd better change his ways.

His good Christian upbringing warred with his erotic feelings for his wife —feelings he'd never felt before for any other woman. He'd tamped them down when he'd casually suggested anal sex to her after they first married, but she'd appeared appalled at the suggestion. He'd tamped down his desires—for seven years he'd done so. Now, he admitted they'd fallen into mundane sex in their marriage—and not very often. It was time to do something about it and he had her to thank for calling it to his attention. He would have preferred it if she had just told him instead of putting him through all that she did this night, but he was glad she had done it.

He looked down at her tenderly, groaning at her ravaged face and took her in his arms. "In another week, this project I'm working on will be done. How about we take a cruise or a nice vacation to somewhere warm?"

Tears slipped from her eyes. "Do you mean it?"

He nodded as a slow grin creased his face. "Yes. But right now, we've more important things to tend to, right?" At her nod and smile he added, "Do you know what I want even more for us?"

"What?" she asked.

"That we never take each other for granted, as I've done with you over the last several months. I'm sorry for that."

Miranda sobbed, stood on tiptoe and wound her arms around his neck. Lord, but her soft curves heated him to his core. Then she set him ablaze when her lips crushed his. He settled his hand on her bare ass and rubbed it in an effort to soothe her. He stepped back, held her arm, and turned her to the side. He shook his head at the sight of her sweet, curvy bottom protruding from the back of her dress as he tried to figure out the sense of it. Then it dawned on him.

"Was this dress made specifically for spanking?"

A charming blush seeped into her cheeks and she nodded even as she tried to escape his hold on her. He kept her in place in front of him. No way was he allowing her to leave now. She'd purchased this particular dress with a spanking in mind. As her husband, it was his responsibility to oblige her. He'd give her plenty of the attention she craved, and then some.

"Then I say it's time we finish off where we left off outside. I'll meet you upstairs in a few minutes."

She bit her lip, her eyes widening in surprise and happiness as she whispered, "Yes, Justin."

He watched her run up the stairs before making his way to the kitchen. Rummaging in a utensil drawer until he found what he'd been searching for. By this night's end, he planned on her ass being the same color as the fire engine red dress she currently wore, but he'd take things slow and easy with her, then build up the spanking with more intensity over time, then make love to her until he'd satisfied both of them. He'd give her exactly what she craved —which he slowly realized wasn't a bad idea.

Purposefully, with wooden spoon in hand, he took the stairs. In their bedroom, he watched her as she leaned against one tall bed poster, keeping her front side to him, her ass tight against the wooden poster. He smiled to himself when her gaze widened on the spoon he held. Slowly, he laid it upon their bed. He was beginning to enjoy this little game between them. He'd been furious when he spanked her out on the front stoop but now all he wanted to do was give her the pleasure she craved, and his full attention.

Justin's small smile lifted into a full-fledged grin. "Don't think you can protect yourself from me. I'm bigger and stronger."

A twinkle entered her eyes. "I don't deny it, but I believe I'm quicker on my feet. And, I'm several years younger than you."

He swept her body a look of distinct disdain. "True, but, in the end, I'll win."

"I'll escape you," she announced with a sniff.

He held up a key. "'Afraid not." He proceeded to lock the door.

Justin enjoyed the astonished look on her face before he entered the bathroom. Returning to the bedroom, he removed his tuxedo jacket and saw her eyes move to the hand that had held the key.

"Tell me you didn't just flush away the key to our room."

"Sorry, but I did. Run all you like. You won't get far. I guarantee you'll tire eventually."

He liked how she kept her distance from him as he continued to undress. He'd removed his jacket, and then unknotted his bowtie, pulling it from around his neck. As he rolled up his sleeves, preparing himself for business, he thoroughly enjoyed the widening of her panic-stricken eyes.

"Worried?" he asked casually.

Her eyes widened further.

Damn, but he was enjoying this foreplay. "You needn't be. You know that I love you and only plan on giving you exactly what you deserve, exactly what you've desired, apparently, for a very long time."

She laughed and scrambled across their bed, landing on her feet on the opposite side. He ambled around the bed toward her, taking his time. Miranda made him feel ten years younger with this cat and mouse chase game. He narrowed his eyes, anticipating her next move, his gaze settling on each luscious curve of her womanly body.

Just after she jumped onto the bed and rolled away, he was on her. As soon as he laid his hands on her waist, holding her down on the bed, she quieted. He released her waist and settled his hands on the bed on either side of her head. Lowering his body to hers, he ground himself against her, and immediately he hardened. Then he kissed her in the way he used to before they married; long, lingering, wet, hot lips meshing together frantically.

Lifting his head, he smiled down at her, thinking how delightful it would be to have her over his knee again. He envisioned her curvy ass held high, still pink from his earlier spanking. He'd been angry then and hadn't enjoyed that spanking but this one he would.

He rose from her, reached down and pulled the ugly red gown from her body, then sat down on the side of the bed. His gaze met hers and his heart lurched when he saw the love in her eyes, and trust. Then she nodded and eased herself over his knee. He picked up the spoon beside him, raised his hand high as he stared down at the canvas he'd be painting again then felt her stiffen across his knees.

"Not hard, Justin, promise me you won't! I'm still sore."

He saw that her ass still blushed a light pink and said, "Sweetheart, I think you can take whatever I dish out. His arm came down twice in rapid succession on each cheek.

She started kicking and screaming even before the first stroke. He delivered light smacks, mixed with an occasional harder stroke. Her ass turned a brighter pink yet he knew, even though she protested, they weren't real protests; she enjoyed this treatment from him, had asked him for it, and damn it if he didn't find himself growing harder beneath her body. He loved how she squirmed across his lap, pressing against his cock.

Satisfaction tore through him when her protests ceased but she continued to writhe on his lap, her intermittent groans mixed with ragged breathing letting him know he'd aroused her.

She loved this kinky sex as she called it and he would oblige her. After tonight, never again would she doubt his love for her. He slowed the strokes, his arm raised in between them, smiling when she stilled in anticipation of the next smack. When it landed, she arched her body, tossed her head back, and groaned aloud. Slowly, enticingly, he slid the side of the spoon between her thighs between spanks, pressing against her clit and rubbing the hard wood against her. He left her gasping with pleasure. Soon her breathing grew raspier, louder, and she groaned aloud as she climaxed.

He repeated the treatment twice more, and when he gauged her entirely spent, her body hanging over his knee, ragged and utterly drenched, he stopped. He sat her up on his knee and kissed her, then fell back on the bed with her in his arms atop him. He pressed her face against his chest, stroked her hair, and murmured, "I love you, you know. Never doubt me on this—or I'll have to punish you."

"Oh, Justin," Miranda sobbed, laughing at the same time. "Please do!"

Justin's heart lurched painfully inside his chest, seeing how happy he'd made her and cursing himself for having been an insensitive, unknowing jerk. He should have seen the signs of her distress at his preoccupation with work, without her having to act out. She shouldn't have had to tell him. He just should have been observant and known.

He rolled them over and pressed her flat on the bed and, with his eyes on hers, he slid down her body until he lay between her legs. Sliding his hands beneath her ass, he raised her to his lips and tongued her clit until she screamed, her body arching high. As she settled down on the bed he saw her chest heaving, heard her panting as she came down and he slid up and lay atop her, his forearms keeping his weight off her. Rubbing his body gently over hers drove her wild and she twisted beneath him. Miranda groaned when he shoved a knee between her legs and ground against her clit.

"Please, Justin! Come inside me!"

"I'm willing to oblige your every wish, baby," he said. He heard the harsh determined tone in his own voice, knowing he was on the brink of an orgasm, but reining himself in to prolong her enjoyment. He had many missed opportunities in loving her that he needed to make up for, and even though she begged him to take her, he knew she'd enjoy and remember this night a long while if he took her slowly, exquisitely. Then he sank with painful slowness inside her lush, wet channel. He stayed there, throbbing, calming himself in an effort not to orgasm too early.

Miranda had other ideas though. He cursed her, then pleaded with her to stop when she tightened her vaginal muscles around his hard cock—until he couldn't hold himself back any longer. With three long thrusts he came, groaning as his cum exploded inside her.

They made love again that night, and again, seemingly not able to get enough of each other. Making up for all of the nights they had missed together.

E leven months later, Justin's bratty wife blessed him with a son. He was proud and pleased, but mostly, now that Miranda wasn't pregnant any longer, he had plans for them. She'd racked up a number of misdemeanors over the past months. Of course, that would mean several sessions over his knees, and over the end of the bed, the leather sofa in the library; not to mention over the spanking horse he'd recently purchased from Thorns and Roses.

He was looking forward to resuming their new life together—to further explore this new spicy frontier upon which they had embarked. Never again would he ignore her. He planned to keep his wife happy and satisfied.

THE END

FIRST TIME

TARA FOX HALL

When a handsome stranger gifts Vicky with a riding crop on her first visit to the local adult bookstore, she hesitantly accepts it along with his dinner invitation. Little does she know the wild passion that Cain will ignite with the first strike of leather against her bare flesh.

FIRST TIME

Vicky stared at the dildos and cockrings on the walls, trying not to flush at the sheer size of some of them. And what was with the colors? There was a rainbow of rubber here. Didn't people want flesh tones, even if the dick inside their body wasn't real? The specialty line in small boxes with high price tags was also bizarre and confusing to her. Why would anyone want a dildo made of glass? The possibilities of it breaking at an ill-timed moment were frightening, to say the least...

"Danette, you'd better fucking do something!" a scruffy man said angrily, approaching the counter. "There's an asshole outside, and he's spitting into my truck. He said I stole his chains, and I never touched a fucking one—"

Vicky flushed redder at the customer's foul language, moving away down the aisle. Why had she come in here? She should've purchased a vibrator online. Deviants frequented adult bookstores. She'd be lucky not to hear cop cars...

"—I'm not going to do anything," Danette said defensively. "He's outside the store."

"It's on your fucking property, and he's already followed me down to the highway and back. Fucking call the cops."

"I'm not calling the cops—"

"—then you're going to have a fight on your hands because that bastard isn't—"

"—Get out of here, now—"

Worried, Vicky apprehensively moved away down the aisle, eyes averted. There was cursing, then the front door of the shop opened, a buzzer sounding.

Relieved the angry man had left, Vicky looked up, her eyes falling on a bunch of leather whips and riding crops. Intrigued, she moved closer, studying them. The whips were all soft leather, and didn't look as if they'd hurt at all, much less do any kind of stimulation. The braided crops looked all business, though. Some crops had heart-shaped tips instead of the usual square riding crop ends, making her smile.

Who wanted to be hit as they had sex? And who wanted to do the hitting? She picked a crop up and looked closer at the label. On it was written "Giddy up! Let's play horsey." Giddy up, indeed, Vicky thought, snorting back laughter.

"First time?" a male voice asked inquisitively.

Vicky jumped, startled, the riding crop threatening to slide from her hands. She grabbed it, then quickly hung the crop back on the hook with a smile, turning to face a well-dressed dark-haired man in a suit, his expression teasing. He was tall and handsome, his outfit not at all what she expected in a place like this. His eyes were to die for: a light honey color that was almost gold. In short, the man looked as though he stepped off the cover of one of the female-targeted sex toy packages.

"Those can be a lot of fun," the man said, inclining his head.

"I'm sure," Vicky replied awkwardly, trying to think of something else to say besides her lustful thoughts.

"No, really," the man continued, stepping closer to the crops. He picked up the one she'd put back. "This one's nice. It's got the traditional tip. Much more satisfying for both parties—"

He must be a sadist, or something. Shudder. "I see," Vicky said, moving away down the aisle.

"Are you looking to give it or get it?" the man teased, smacking the crop lightly against his hand with a "Whap!"

"Neither," Vicky said primly, moving away past the blow up dolls to the costumes, her eyes adverted.

"I can only hope you'll change your mind," the man said politely. He smiled, then walked away in the opposite direction.

Relieved, Vicky looked through some costumes, then at the toys. Finally selecting a small vibrator, she took it to the cash register. The man rang it up, and put it in a bag, taking her cash. But when he handed her that bag, he handed her another larger bag with it.

"That's not mine," Vicky said in confusion, handing it back.

"No refunds or exchanges," the guy said, holding up his hands. "Thank you for shopping Porn World."

Vicky went outside. After looking right and left, she opened the mystery bag. Inside were the riding crop and a note. "I'd be honored to help you discover satisfaction," she read aloud, flushing. Written underneath was a telephone number with the single name, Cain.

Unsettled, Vicky stuffed the crop and note deep into the bag, and rolled it up. She stashed it under her driver's seat, climbed in, then peeled out.

That whole next week, Vicky would take out the crop and examine it right before bed, her hands sliding up and down the smooth leather, the nylon reinforced shaft almost silky under her fingers. When she used it for trial on her forearm, the leather tip stung slightly, but didn't hurt or leave a mark. Yet what she enjoyed most was the attention-riveting whap of the leather hitting flesh.

Her dreams each night were filled with the handsome stranger, Cain, of him coming to her naked, undressing her slowly, his lips trailing down her skin as he removed each piece of clothing. When at last she was naked, Cain would offer her the riding crop with a languid smile. But always, as Vicky reached to accept it, she would wake instantly, the rush 'of elation from the dream smothered by her too real disappointment and mounting sexual frustration.

The solution was easy, Vicky knew. Contacting Cain could make her fantasy come true, if she but dared call the number. He obviously had experience in the art of seduction, and some experience with BDSM. What worried Vicky was how reality would compare to her fantasy. Yet if she didn't contact Cain, could she bear not knowing what might have happened if she had?

On Friday, Vicky gathered her courage and dialed the number. A male voice answered on the first ring.

"Cain."

Say it before you lose your nerve. "Hi," Vicky began, already flustered. "I'm Vicky. You gave me a riding crop about a week ago—"

"The girl from Porn World," Cain said with interest. "Have you decided to wet your toes?"

"Yes," Vicky said breathlessly, a thrill running through her. "How does this work?"

"We should meet first for dinner," Cain replied. "How about the Italian place in town? What time is good for you? I'm happy to pick you up, but understand if you'd rather drive yourself."

Vicky wanted to be able to leave, just in case Cain wasn't all she hoped he was. "I'll meet you there. Eight?"

"Perfect, Vicky. See you there."

Vicky waited at the table, nervously sipping water. Where was Cain? She had been early, but it was now five minutes after eight.

"Excuse me," a waiter said, appearing at her arm. "Are you Miss Vicky?"

"Yes," Vicky offered, curious.

"Please come with me," the waiter said, taking her coat. "This way."

Vicky followed him through the semi-crowded room to the etched glass double doors at the side, her interest aroused. The waiter pushed open one of the doors, revealing a single cozy table lit by candlelight, a man playing piano, and Cain, who was busy pouring a bottle of red wine into two large goblets.

"Ah!" Cain said, setting down the opened bottle. "There you are. Please have a seat, Vicky, and look over the menu. Jean-Paul knows my preferences already."

Did he? Vicky thought but didn't say. She obediently sat, and opened the menu, looking at the varied dishes. After a short time, she selected the eggplant parmigiana, and handed the menu to the waiter, who left the room.

"To a budding friendship, if not more," Cain said, raising his glass. Vicky raised hers too, offering a smile. Delicately, their glasses clinked, then both sipped lightly before putting their wine aside.

Vicky looked over at the piano player, who was playing something that was light and relaxing on the upright instrument, instead of the seductive music she had expected.

"To make you at ease," Cain said, leaning back in his chair. "You were very nervous in the store. I don't want you to be nervous here tonight with me."

Immediately, Vicky was reminded of all the dildos in a row on the store shelf, her fantasies of Cain, and the smile he'd worn while offering her the crop, so similar to the one he was wearing now. Her flush began light, then deepened, her face burning. Hopefully Cain hadn't noticed in the dim light. "It was the setting," she said, as calmly as she could. "I don't go to adult stores usually."

"Why did you go this time?" Cain asked.

Vicky reached for her water, and drank some slowly, then put the glass down. She looked at Cain, then away.

"You can tell me," Cain continued. "I was intrigued before, but your reluctance to tell me is captivating. I must know now."

"This is embarrassing," Vicky murmured, flushing again.

"I'm not pressuring you for more than what your sexual tastes run to," Cain said, as if he were discussing the menu items. "I'm here tonight because I would like to have an encounter with you, if not several. But I care very much that what I would like to do would be something you would be interested in, too."

Vicky looked at her lap, trying to contain her blush along with her disappointment. "You want sex," she said softly.

"Don't you?" Cain replied gently, moving his chair closer, so that he sat by her side. He took her hand in his. "I'm not looking for a one night stand, Vicky. I want a relationship with a woman who will join me in my fantasies, share her own with me, and enjoy both. I'd like to discover if you can be that woman."

The closeness of Cain and the feel of his hand in hers already had Vicky shifting in her seat from desire. She tried to clear her head and focus on his words. "Will we meet just for sex, then?"

"Ah," Cain said, nodding. "You think I'm looking for someone to play with, then send off when I'm done."

The tone of his words was hurt, so hurt that Vicky was surprised enough to look up into his face. His expression closed fast over the hurt, and he went to move his chair back to the other side of the table.

Vicky grabbed Cain's arm, stopping him. "I didn't mean to offend you," she said quickly. "I just want more than sex. I had that for the last year…and I finally ended it, because it was obvious that was all he wanted me for."

Cain paused, then sat down, taking her hand in his. "You were the Other Woman."

Vicky nodded her smile bitter. "I can't say I didn't know it from the beginning, because I did. But I thought that there was going to be more, that things would change. But he liked our arrangement just as it was." She faced Cain, hope and somberness in her eyes. "I don't want to go through that again, even if you don't have someone else."

"I don't have someone else," Cain assured, squeezing her hand. "My previous lover broke off with me a month ago."

A month ago? Vicky had been alone for close to seven months now. Was Cain really ready to start something new? "What happened?"

"She wanted more than what I could give her," Cain said delicately. "Her tastes changed, and she no longer liked…what I liked." He took his glass, and drank a swallow of wine. "What do you want out of life that you are sure of?"

Taken aback, Vicky reached for her own wine, and took a large sip. Carefully, she placed it down on the table, unsure if the conversation was making her bold, or the wine was the real culprit. "I want to be happy, to have someone that loves me, and enjoy every day I have," she answered. "That's all I'm sure of at this moment, Cain."

Cain smiled, lifting his glass. "Those are exactly my feelings, too, Vicky. Are you ready to eat?"

The waiter opened the double doors, and brought in their food. Vicky began eating as if famished, devouring the entire entrée. Cain also ate eagerly, their conversation limited though his chair remained close to hers. Dessert was also quickly decided on, and shared: a massive piece of cheesecake with strawberries that was just delightful.

When the waiter came to take their plates away, the piano player closed the cover on the instrument, gave them a smile, then left with the waiter. Cain poured the rest of the bottle into the two wineglasses, and again regarded Vicky. "Are you ready to tell me your fantasies now?"

The good meal coupled with the music had relaxed Vicky, and her nervousness was long gone. "I wasn't in the shop looking for exotic stuff," she said to Cain. "I just wanted something a little bit fun and new to try. My toys were ones I'd had for a while, and I was feeling bored. I wanted to see what else was out there."

"Why not try the internet, then?" Cain said. "It is definitely more anonymous."

"Because you can't tell how something feels until you hold it in your hands," Vicky retorted with a laugh. "Some toys look good, but they feel or smell terrible. I have standards for what I allow inside my body."

"Do I meet your standards?" Cain asked huskily. His lips brushed Vicky's ear, then slid lower, kissing the side of her neck.

Vicky took a long shuddering breath, then turned, her lips meeting his eagerly. Their kiss exploded, lips parting as tongues darted in though open lips to lick and taste.

Finally, they separated, breathing hard.

"I think that answers you," Vicky murmured sexily. "But I'll say it anyway. Yes, you meet my standards, Cain."

"Ah, but I think I should be made to pass your personal test, Vick," Cain said casually. He took her hand, and rested it on his groin. "Go ahead. I await your full inspection."

Vicky's heart was already pounding, and it speeded up further at the throbbing heat under her hand. *Dare she? No one was here...*

She carefully unzipped his bulging fly, then reached into Cain's pants, moving his erection outside the cloth to stand. The sheer size of his penis was impressive the smooth flesh purpled and engorged with blood. Vicky slipped her hands over the skin, rubbing the tip with her thumb. Cain let out groan, his hips moving up slightly.

"Very nice," she said huskily. Vicky moved back her chair, then knelt gracefully. Carefully she leaned in, then began to work the head of Cain's rod with her hands, while running her tongue up and down the sides of the shaft. Almost at once, fluid began to leak from the tip, Cain's breathing becoming eager, panting.

Vicky, moved back, then smiled up at Cain. "But there is only one test that matters, you know."

Cain didn't look away from her lustful eyes, the heat of his direct gaze matching hers in intensity. "If I can get you there." He smiled. "Go ahead, Vick. Try me."

"This chair's too flimsy," Vicky said, her gaze darting around the room, her need was suddenly urgent as she saw the leather overstuffed wingback chair. "That chair will work. Hurry!"

Cain moved to the leather chair, sitting back with a groan as he slipped a condom from his pocket. He slid it over his erection, then Vicky straddled him, easing aside her thong panties for the thick flesh to penetrate her. A loud moan escaped her lips as Cain's erection eased into her.

This was no toy. This was real flesh. God, it felt so good!

Almost at once, Vicky began to rock, her frustration of the whole last week flooding her, her desire for climax insatiable. Each movement of her hips brought her sweet torture and building frenzy as she moved faster, her only thought her own pleasure. Cain cupped her ass, pulling her closer for each thrust, his lips devouring her throat as her head went back in a loud scream as the orgasm burst upon her.

Vicky sagged into Cain, her parted lips slack in satisfaction, breathing hard.

"I take it I passed?" Cain said seductively, kissing her forehead.

"Oh yeah," Vicky sighed, taking his face in her hands, and kissing his lips deeply. "But why didn't you come, too?"

"One orgasmic cry we can talk our way out of," Cain said with a laugh. "But not two. We'd best be going now, before we're discovered."

He helped Vicky stand, as she reluctantly released him, then folded the used condom up into a tissue, and slipped it in his pocket. Dropping some cash on the table, Cain grabbed their coats, then took her hand and they hurried outside, bursting into laughter as soon as they were outside.

"I've never done anything like that before," Vicky said, twining her arms around Cain's neck. "When will I see you again?"

"We didn't really discuss your fantasies, or mine," Cain said, holding her. "Are you game to try without knowing what you're signing on for? I'll understand if you aren't."

All Vicky knew was she wanted more of Cain, no matter what she had to do to get him. "Yes."

"Then come to 236 Fenton Rd tomorrow night at eight," Cain said seductively, kissing her earlobe. "And bring my present, Vick."

Promptly at eight, Vicky eagerly knocked on the large wooden door. A butler answered, then showed her inside.

Cain strode in a few minutes later, another waiter behind him bearing a bottle of wine, and two glasses. "Hello, Vicky. Would you care for a drink before we adjourn to the bedroom?"

I'll need one for courage, Vicky thought. "Please."

The butler poured. Cain handed a glass of red wine to Vicky, taking the other for himself. "To first times," he said, clinking her glass with his. "And new discoveries."

Vicky drained her glass from nervousness, then set it down. Cain took a long sip from his, set it down, and then took Vicky's hand. "Come, my dear."

He led her up a staircase to the second floor, then into a large bedroom, the king size bed a plush oval of pillows and satin sheets. Vicky stared, worried suddenly that she'd bitten off too much to chew. What would he do to her?

"Relax," Cain said, sliding off her coat. "Nothing is going to happen tonight that you don't want to happen, Vicky. In fact, it's crucial that you tell me at once if anything is less than perfect for you." He kissed her cheek. "Most exotic sexual first times are dismal failures, marked forever after as an activity never to be tried again." He brushed her lips lightly with his own. "This first time with you, I just want to whet your appetite. I want you to yearn for more."

Vicky smiled, then began to take off her clothes. Surprisingly, Cain stopped her, taking her face in his hands and kissing her. The pressure of his lips was sweet, yet also invigorating, stirring her ardor even as her heart beat quickened. Vicky kissed back, winding her arms around his neck. Cain kissed her hungrily, his hands sliding down from her face to her shoulders, enfolding her. His mouth kissed lower, sucking gently on her throat. Vicky let out a moan, clutching him. Cain's hands slid to her waist, then lower, to cup her bottom, squeezing slightly. Vicky moaned again.

With his right hand, Cain rubbed Vicky's cheek through her pants, then tapped her smartly with the flat of his hand. Vicky jerked, startled.

"I'm not punishing," Cain said hungrily, still kissing her throat. "You're a good girl, Vicky. But I need more."

Vicky's breaths came faster. "What do you need?"

"Your breast," Cain whispered sexily. "Undo your shirt."

Vicky unbuttoned her blouse, then opened the front, revealing her white bra.

Cain kissed down her hot skin, nuzzling his face between her breasts as he rubbed her buttocks with his hands. Then he moved his lips lower, putting his mouth to the fabric and sucking gently, teasing her nipples through the white lace. Vicky moaned, tried to pull him close.

Cain spanked her again gently. "No, no. Be a good girl, Vicky," he murmured, again kissing her neck.

"Please, don't stop," Vicky moaned. "Please—"

"Lift them both out for me," Cain whispered in her ear. "Those are beautiful breasts you have, Vicky. I want to see them on display." He sucked her earlobe, then traced it with his tongue. "Touch your nipples and make them hard for me."

Panting, Vicky reached down with her hands, lifting her breasts out of her bra. She rubbed both nipples with her fingers, making the flesh redden and tighten.

"Perfect," Cain said. He bent his head, his mouth engulfing one nipple. The warm sensuous shock of it made Vicky cried out, her shudder delicious as Cain continued to suck and tease her swollen flesh.

Cain sucked gently, his tongue probing and licking until Vicky was mad from wanting. With a groan, her hands slipped down, reaching for the front of his jeans, her fingers yanking down the zipper, eager to caress his swollen erection.

Cain spanked her again, the slap of his hand through her pants more commanding. "No. Be a good girl, Vicky. You don't get to touch me yet. This is all about you, honey."

"Please," she said, kissing his throat, and his lips. "I want you, Cain—"

"And I want you," he replied, kissing her long and passionately. "But you're still going to wait."

Cain bent his head again to the other breast, feeding and tonguing. Vicky went crazy, moaning, her hands clenching and unclenching. Minute by minute, the yearning built until it was all consuming. In desperation, she slipped her hands into her own pants.

Cain's hand caught hers, his mouth moving back from her glistening nipple. He looked up at her, then shook his head slightly. "Two warnings are all you get."

He picked her up and over his shoulder, then set her down on the bed, flipping her carefully onto her stomach. Vicky blinked in disbelief as he bound first one wrist, then the other, the chains attached to both clinking slightly. Cain pulled them tight, taking up the slack, Vicky's body now spread-eagled on the bed face down. Carefully, Cain pulled off Vicky's shoes, socks, and pants.

"Hey," she said loudly, fear taking the place of passion. "Untie me. I don't want—"

The riding crop came down, smacking flat against her bare ass. Vicky shrieked, then began to scream.

"Shh, now." Instantly, Cain lay down beside her, his light kisses moving down over her naked hip, then onto the light red mark on her white skin. Vicky's scream cut off, her fear wavering.

"You need to be punished for not waiting," Cain teased, still kissing her lower back, his hands caressing her soft buns. "When you tell me you're sorry, I'll stop."

"Why, you son of a—"

The riding crop came down again, this time hard. Vicky let out a cry, then swore.

"No foul language." The riding crop came down again with a whap.

"Stop it!" Vicky said angrily. "I want you to stop!"

"Say you're sorry."

"No, I—"

The riding crop came down again twice, one whap on each creamy white bun. Vicky shuddered, her flesh beginning to smart, her heart racing.

Ten more times the crop whapped her buttocks, the flesh reddening.

"Stop," Vicky cried, tears in her eyes. "I'm sorry! I'm sorry!"

Cain put aside the crop, then took off his shirt. He crawled onto the bed, then patted her reddened cheeks gently, his hand sliding lower. Vicky shuddered, then let out a cry of longing as Cain penetrated her, his deft fingers manipulating and stimulating her clitoris as she writhed on the bed.

"That feels good, doesn't it?" Cain whispered, his other hand stroking up her naked back, then splaying possessively. "Tell me if it does."

"Please, yes," Vicky moaned. "I want you."

"I know you do," he said lovingly. "But I want to make sure you've learned your lesson. Are you going to behave?"

"Yes," Vicky groaned.

Cain slapped her ass, the sharp clap bringing a cry from Vicky. "Say it!"

"I'll behave! I'll behave!"

"Good girl," Cain said approvingly. He massaged her swollen cheeks, then untied her hands. "Sit there, while I get ready. And no touching yourself."

Vicky nodded, eagerly watching him slide off his jeans, then pull down the condom tightly over his engorged penis. With a sigh, Cain rolled onto his back, his tight abs rippling, then beckoned to Vicky.

Eagerly she straddled him, moaning contentedly as his hard flesh pushed up into hers. At once, she began to rock hard, throwing her head back.

"No," Cain cautioned, rapping her buns again with his hands. Vicky stopped instantly, her chest heaving, her eyes wild with raw need.

"Slow," Cain said, again dipping his head to her breast, the taut flesh sliding between his lips. "Slow and deep—"

Vicky groaned, then pushed down, sliding the last inches of his stiff penis inside her. She began to rock slowly, each thrust of her pelvis on his stimulating her, rubbing her clit as his thick shaft stroked her, the movement making her cry out with pleasure.

Cain groaned, his hands reaching to cup Vicky's buttocks, gently guiding and massaging. As she stroked his penis with her wet warmth, he began to spank her gently in rhythm, his grunts louder as he approached orgasm.

Vicky gasped, then let out a loud scream, throwing back her head with abandon as her climax washed through her. Under her, Cain thrust up hard, matching her thrust for thrust as her body pulsated around his, the last squeeze of her vagina bringing his come in a spurting flood; his triumphant yell deafening.

Cain thrust up a few more times, his satisfied groans weakening. Gently, he guided Vicky down on him, laying her sated body on his.

He gently pushed some damp hair from her face, then brushed her lips with his. "How was your first time?"

"Wonderful," Vicky said, giving a sigh of satisfaction. "There's just one problem."

"What's that?" Cain asked, curious.

"I'll need a second," Vicky teased, her throaty voice filled with heat.

Cain smiled. "When?"

"The sooner the better."

Cain kissed her, then spanked her bottom gently. "Then how do you feel about another trip to Porn World? We've just scratched the surface, Vicky." He rubbed her nipple, tracing his finger around it once, then pulling gently, wresting another cry from her. "There's so much more I want to show you."

"I'm game," she purred sexily. "Tomorrow night." She reached down beside the bed, grabbing up the crop. "Right now, I need my steed."

Cain smiled widely, then kissed her passionately. "Are you going to be good?" he whispered huskily.

"I'm going to be better than good," she answered, reclining back on the sheets, crop in her hand. With her other hand, she beckoned. "Come here, stud."

"So ready to switch from dominated to dominatrix, are you?" Cain murmured. He yanked the whip from her grasp. "I think not, Vicky."

Vicky shifted uneasily, unsure of what she wanted. She had enjoyed the role-playing with Cain, but how far was she willing to go? Did she really want to dominate Cain? Her dreams of him had always ended before anything had actually happened.

"Turn over," Cain ordered. "You've earned another spanking, missy."

"Just a moment," Vicky stalled, standing up. "I've got to go to the bathroom."

Instead of Cain protesting, he just nodded. "Hurry back."

Vicky darted into the bathroom, then locked the door behind her. Her emotions a tumult, she sagged down on the toilet seat, considering her options.

Cain had showed her some amazing sex. But that wasn't enough to ease her mind. Her harsh Catholic upbringing railed against what they had just done, telling her it was abnormal and twisted. Even though Vicky knew that wasn't true, she still wasn't sure if Cain was the kind of bed partner she wanted. How much of his controlled domination was real, and how much was the role he was playing?

Whichever explanation was true, she wanted more. And there was no time like the present.

Vicky opened the bathroom door, then went over to Cain, waiting in bed.

"You said there is a first time for everything, Cain," Vicky said. "Tonight, it's for you to try making the switch from master to servant."

"Being dominated has never held any appeal for me," he said politely.

"It didn't for me, until you," Vicky said simply. "Try it just once. That's all I'm asking. You wanted to know my fantasy, but the truth is, I'm not sure if this is something I really want, or just something I want to try. Please, help me figure out which."

Cain's expression was skeptical, but he nodded. "Go ahead, Vick."

An instant thrill went through Vicky. "Lie on your back with your legs apart," she said. "I want to see everything."

Cain obediently got into position. But his penis was soft, clearly unwilling.

Vicky fastened Cain with the four cuffs, tying him spread eagle to the bed. She took in his hard muscles, his lean frame, and his more than ample equipment. Picking up the riding crop, she held it in her hand, unsure of what to do. Did she really want to discipline Cain? The thought of spanking him made her feel ridiculous…

"Anytime, darlin'," Cain drawled.

At once, his insolent tone showed her what to do. "Silence," Vicky said, bringing the crop down on Cain with a sharp whap. Cain hissed in surprise more than pain, and narrowed his eyes.

"This is my night to teach you patience," Vicky said. She grabbed for her discarded shirt, winding it with sudden inspiration. Carefully, she slipped the blindfold over Cain's eyes, then laying the crop aside she began tonguing Cain's nipples, enjoying the small nubs of flesh as they hardened in her mouth.

"That isn't doing anything for me," Cain began. A sharp whap sounded, as the crop came down again, eliciting another hiss of pain.

"It's doing something for me," Vicky said gleefully. "You will lie there and submit. When you are able to be silent for a few moments, you'll get your reward."

Cain lapsed into silence.

Vicky played with his nipples with her tongue, then moved lower, kissing his taut abs as she rubbed his nipples. Cain remained silent, though she could feel the tenseness in his body. With sudden inspiration, Vicky squeezed his nipples hard. Cain flinched, but kept his silence.

"Very good," she said huskily, moving lower. "You can have your reward." She licked the soft length of his penis, feeling it jerk as it began elongating, and hardening from her simple caress.

Cain let out an eager sound.

Vicky removed the blindfold, then brandished her whip." No sounds, not even a murmur, or I stop. Understood?"

Cain nodded, his chest heaving. His erection was standing proudly now, bobbing slightly, the tip already moist.

Vicky smiled seductively then began to play. At first, she merely teased Cain, doing all she could to elicit any groan from his lips with teasing kisses, and stroking tongue. But as the silence stretched and he remained quiet, she upped her game, engulfing the head of his hard dick in her warm mouth, tugging lightly as she licked the slit leaking his excitement.

Cain began to move, at first gently, then more forcefully, his silence in stark contrast to his contracting body and rapid, eager panting. With long sure strokes, Vicky pleasured him, his movements regular and restrained by the barest inch, his hands clasping and unclasping.

Vicky gave the moist throbbing shaft one last teasing kiss, then slipped the head out, her bedroom eyes looking demurely up at Cain. "Ready to come?"

"Yes," Cain rasped out gutturally.

Vicky unlocked Cain's cuffs, then laid down, crop in hand. She beckoned with a single finger and a slow smile. "Come to me."

Cain grabbed a condom from beside the bed, and put it on with shaking fingers. As soon as it was on, he rolled over onto her, swiftly moving her legs apart so he could penetrate her. Pushing up with both hands, Cain drove deep, arching his back as he contracted his buttock, pushing in as deep as he could, a long wavering cry of satiation escaping his lips.

A sharp whap of the crop hitting his thighs rang out. Cain paused, a shudder running through him.

"Slow," Vicky warned. "I want to come, Cain." She trailed the crop down his chest, then tapped him lightly with it. 'It's difficult for me to come in this position. If you can do it, I'll surrender the crop to you. If you can't…" Vicky tapped him a little harder on his bare left buttock with a sharp whap.

Cain smiled, then began to move.

Within a few strokes, Vicky groaned in pleasure, even as she grumbled that she should have set Cain a harder task. Already she felt the first stirrings of orgasm, and he had just started to move. Deliberately, to lengthen the encounter, she dipped her hips, moving the contact point of her body with his. The pleasurable sensation dimmed slightly, and she smiled to be once again in control.

"Oh no, mistress," Cain said, moving his hands beneath her hips. With a deft pull, he moved her back into position, restoring the contact of his root and her clit. At once the pleasure hit again in waves. Vicky groaned, and her desire to resist withered, all her thought now on attaining the orgasm that waited just before her.

Cain gave her a knowing smile, then bore down slightly, moving just a little differently. At once, the burgeoning feeling of imminent climax grew unbearable. Vicky groaned, then thrust up, no longer able to remain motionless. At once, white hot fire lanced through her core, her body contracting around Cain's as she began to scream, his thrusting suddenly fast and hard as she clutched him closer, relief and ecstasy mixed into one as she came.

Cain thrust until her cries weakened, then gently took the crop from her lax fingers. "I so wanted to spank you for your daring," he teased, sliding it over her breasts, then tapping softly. "But I loved giving you that fantasy, Vic." He kissed her parted lips gently, then drew back. "You aren't a Dom, but you do show potential, I admit. It would be a shame to ignore the possibilities." He moved her onto her stomach, then entered her from behind, her groan at being filled quickly replaced by cries of pleasure as he stroked her hard and fast.

"But remember—"

His hand came down on her tensed buttock, making her flesh sing and her cry of pleasure louder.

"—I am master here—"

Another light slap landed, making Vicky cry out again.

"—say it!"

"You're my master," Vicky moaned.

Another slap, this one harder. "Louder!"

"You're my master!"

Cain tensed, then groaned, his hips vibrating as he let loose, his hands clenched on Vicky's hips. Slowing, he groaned again, then pulled out, carefully removing the condom. Without his support, Vicky collapsed, rolling over in bliss to sprawl on her side, panting hard and fast. She looked up at Cain lazily as he lowered himself down by her side, then enfolded her in his arms.

"Well, I liked it," Vicky said when she regained her breath. "I think you did, too."

"While I did like parts of this, my tastes are unchanged," Cain admitted. "But you're right that I needed to try this. I'm afraid this will be my lone foray into being disciplined though, Vicky."

Vicky pouted, irked that Cain was unwilling to switch roles, as she had done. "But what about me? While I love what you do to me, I don't want to give up the fun of being the one on top, so to speak."

Cain laughed, then kissed her cheek. "You won't have to. I have a friend that would be glad to have you whip him as much as you wanted. In fact, he would beg you for it, Vick."

Vicky felt a thrill run down into her loins. "Are you sure? You um…you wouldn't mind?"

Cain shook his head. "Don't think I'm being coy, or that I do this lightly. I don't introduce my good friends to just anyone. But I like you, Vicky. I don't want this to be a one night stand, or even just a few nights, as I said at dinner last night." He kissed her hand. "But you haven't said what you want. Do you want me for more than tonight? Do you want a relationship with me? It's okay if you don't."

"I'm not sure," Vicky said honestly. "I'm too new to all this. Do I like what we did? Yes. Am I sure of what else I might be open to? No."

Cain smiled. "Then what I'd suggest is a few more nights before you make a decision. You should never commit until you are certain exactly what you are signing on for. And I'm happy to help you discover your likes and dislikes."

The night had been amazing, Vicky thought. Maybe she wouldn't like everything they would try, but her appetite for exploring this new frontier had been whetted. There was no way she was walking away now. "I'm free next week," Vicky said, thinking quickly. "Are you?"

"I can only wait until tomorrow," Cain said sexily. "I can arrange to be free then. How about you?"

"Yes," Vicky said eagerly, nodding once. "I'll be here." She smiled, then kissed him, withdrawing only to snuggle close with a satiated sigh.

THE END

THE SECOND SESSION

TARA FOX HALL

Her desire whetted, Vicky accepts one of Cain's friends into their bed, eager to switch roles from submissive to aggressor. But in her quest to dominate the brawny, muscular Brick, Vicky gives into desire, requiring Cain to administer some well-deserved correction.

THE SECOND SESSION

"God, just like that!" Brick moaned. "Please, don't stop!"

The girl atop him smiled, her long black hair hiding her like a cloak, her fingers reaching down under their joined bodies to grab his ass, her long nails digging in. Brick gasped at the sensation, then felt himself ejaculate, the sweet release tearing a shout of raw pleasure from him as he bucked again and again...

Brick bolted awake, his heart pounding, his skin covered with sweat. A glance at the clock said he'd slept only five hours since coming off his shift at the hospital. Brick took several deep breaths, then relaxed back onto the bed, irritated.

Why had he gone to bed so early after watching that porn video? This is what always happened when he got excited and didn't do anything about it. He looked down, his proud penis standing at attentive salute. Well, there was nothing for it but to...

The phone rang. It wasn't the landline number the hospital would call, but his cell; his private number, one only his friends knew. That meant he had to take it, no matter if he had a raging erection or not.

Brick leaned over with a grunt, and grabbed the cell phone from the nightstand. "This better be good."

"It will be," a male voice teased. "Unless you've decided you don't want to join in on any more of my sessions, Brick."

Please, God, let Cain be in the middle of one of them! That was just what he needed. "Maybe. What did you have in mind? And when?"

"What do you like to do best?" Cain teased. "There was a reason I called you, first, Brick. Now come over immediately…if you want to come, that is—"

Brick didn't have to be asked twice. "Do I need to bring anything?"

"Just your enthusiasm for being dominated. See you soon."

Not soon enough. "I'll be right there."

Brick arrived at Cain's house a half hour later, his steps quick and bouncy as he leapt eagerly up the steps and rang the doorbell. Tonight was going to be great. Any nights Brick spent at Cain's house always were.

They'd become friends quite by accident, meeting at a local bar one night. Brick had just broken up with his girlfriend, and was looking for some male bonding and a drink. Cain…well, Cain had been looking for a playmate.

Brick had noticed Cain as soon as he walked into the bar. While he'd never looked at a man in his life with lust, there was no way to be breathing and not appreciate Cain's attributes. Those gold eyes everyone seemed to go for, coupled with his dark hair and perfect body made him an instant hit with the girls at the bar that night. Cain had had three or four sitting by him when Brick had walked in.

Not that Brick wasn't eye-catching himself. His six-foot frame wasn't just fit with lean muscle, it was rock hard with it. Brick put in a lot of work keeping it that way, too. It wasn't easy. That was bullshit on those exercise gadget infomercials; Brick saw a lot of them, getting up an hour early each day to put in a full workout before a quick shower, then heading off to work. But his job as an X-ray technician kept him busy all day and usually most weekday nights, too. Using various machines to give X-rays had always been a worthwhile career to Brick, but it wasn't the kind of thing to get his heart pumping. And Brick intended never to look middle aged, even if thirty was receding slowly in the rearview mirror…

"Lost in thought?" Cain asked, coming up behind him with his car keys in his hand. He unlocked the door, then pushed it open. "Come on in."

"Remembering the night we met," Brick said with a grin, as he followed Cain inside. "It was more than luck finding you there that night."

"Yes," Cain said, returning the grin. "We both found what we were really looking for, a friend who shared our common interest." He snorted. "You were so uncomfortable."

Brick nodded, shrugging. He'd been shocked and surprised when Cain mentioned a possible threesome, if not more, and asked him what kind of sex he enjoyed. "Well, we were talking about my girlfriend and how she left me—"

"—because you weren't ready to settle down," Cain finished, nodding. He put down the black plastic bag, and went to the liquor cabinet. "Scotch?"

Brick shook his head. "I'm too revved to want to do any downers. Speaking of which, who did you set up for us tonight?"

"Someone special," Cain purred, pouring himself a small straight scotch. He put the bottle aside, then sipped it, turning to face Brick. "Her name is Vicky. We met just a few weeks ago. We got together just last night—"

"She had to consider it?" Brick teased. "You're losing your touch."

"Wiseass," Cain said good-naturedly. "I haven't lost a thing. Vicky is just new to this. But she has a taste for dominating, as well as being dominated. You know I prefer to be the dominant partner, and—"

"—and I don't," Brick said, nodding once. "This sounds great." His forehead creased. "But is she open to me joining you two? I don't want to crash."

Cain nodded. "She said she was, when I broached this little ménage-a-trio to her last night. But I want you to remember she's new to this. So make sure she's okay with something before you do it. And if I tell you to go slow, I mean the level right before stop. Got it?"

Brick nodded. "Got it."

The doorbell rang.

"And there she is," Cain said with a smile. "Time to play."

———

Vicky was led into the hallway by the butler. She gave him her coat. "Is Cain here?"

"Yes," the butler answered. "Please wait here, if you would, ma'am. He'll be right down." The man bowed. "Have a good night, Miss Vicky."

"Thanks, I will," Vicky said, sounding much more certain than she was. As she watched the butler walk off, she felt a chill. Rubbing her bare arms, she sat on a nearby-overstuffed chair, and tried to stay calm.

Cain's request to have another person join them for sex had appalled her at first. Her first thought was that he was already bored with her. She'd only begun seeing him last week, their first date culminating with a sexual encounter. Their first foray into exotic sex had only been last night. What was she getting herself into?

Vicky reasoned that Cain's proposal wasn't as sordid as it sounded. Cain and she were planning dinners a few nights this coming week, to get to know one another better. They had had a long lunch just this afternoon, since it was a Saturday. She and Cain had a lot in common. Both of their lives were already close to bursting with their careers. Both of them had tried the normal dating scene before and not found anyone they liked beyond a second date. Both of them had families that were supportive, but not close, the kind that didn't demand a visit at the holidays and were happy with a card and a gift basket. In short, they made a good match, she and Cain. This wasn't just a hook up; at least it wasn't to her. And if Cain wanted just to hook up, he wouldn't have bothered to see her for lunch or plan dinners, because he wouldn't have needed to do either for her to have come to him tonight.

Vicky admitted brazenly to herself that she'd continue to see Cain even if theirs became just a physical relationship. What he did to her felt too good not to want it as much as she could get it. And while she was leery about another person joining in, she rationalized that with Cain promising it would be a male, not a female, she had every reason to be excited. How many girls got to have that fantasy? And tonight, she was going to see if her fantasies matched the real thing…

"Hi, Vick," Cain said, coming down the stairs. "How's my girl?"

"Ready and waiting," Vicky said boldly. She looked over Cain's shoulder to the brawny man behind him, noting the blatant interest in the man's bright blue eyes. "Hello."

"This is Brick," Cain said politely. "Brick, this is my girlfriend, Vicky."

"Hi," Brick said, taking her hand in his and kissing it. "I'm excited to meet you, and to be here tonight."

Vicky blinked, flushing slightly at the sheer size of Brick, his spiky short dark blond hair, and the bulging biceps and chest that stretched the confines of his shirt. It looked as if one flex would rip open the straining cloth easily. "It's good to meet you."

"He's not what you expected," Cain said in a wicked tone, walking around them and continuing to the stairway. "But you'll enjoy him, Vick, I promise. Would you both come with me into the bedroom?"

Flashing a smile, Brick offered Vicky his arm. Vicky took it, then walked upstairs and into the room, as Cain shut the door behind them.

They were in utter darkness. For a moment, Vicky felt a flash of fear, then she shook it off. So what if this was a different room than last night? Tonight was going to be a new experience, one she couldn't wait to discover.

Cain turned on a single dim light, lit a few candles in wrought iron floor stands, and began taking off his shirt, his dark vee of chest hair appearing in the flickering light. Vicky longed to put her hands on him, but instead looked over at Brick, wondering what she was supposed to do.

Cain came over to Vicky, his chest bared. He unbuttoned just the top few buttons of her blouse, then pushed back the collar, exposing her cleavage.

"I'm so glad you wore what I bought for you," Cain purred. "You look ravishing, Vick." He lightly ran his fingertips over the tops of her breasts affectionately, then embraced her, his kisses trailing up from her breasts to her neck.

"Take off his clothes," he whispered in Vicky's ear. "But do it slowly." He kissed her earlobe. "And tease him a little, if you know what I mean." Cain drew back, then slowly turned Vicky to face Brick, who had moved forward and was now standing directly before her.

Vicky's gaze roamed over Brick, taking in his muscles. She had never been with a man like this. Cain was in shape and toned, but this man had sheer power and strength easily twice over. What would he be like? Brick's expression showed avid hunger already seething to erupt. Would he be forceful, or rough? If she asked him to stop what he was doing, would he?

"Touch him, Vick," Cain whispered throatily. "He is dying to feel your hands on him."

Vicky put her hands on Brick tentatively, and began undoing his shirt. Cain began kissing her neck, murmuring encouragement.

Vicky finished unbuttoning the shirt, then slid it open, revealing Brick's washboard abs and large chest muscles sculpted in relief by the dancing shadows of the candlelight. Vicky let out a groan, then put her hands on warn skin, feeling the hard muscle reflexively bunch under her palms. Brick grunted in pleasure, but made no move to touch her.

Vicky ran her hands up Brick's chest, then pushed the shirt off his shoulders, revealing his impressive physique. Vicky leaned in close, and began to kiss down Brick's chest, her tongue licking his warm, salty skin. Brick groaned, clenching his fists, but didn't move.

Vicky came to Brick's pants, then slowly undid them, yanking out his belt. She pushed down the heavy denim to pool on the carpet, revealing Brick's firm erection through his tight jockey shorts. With a careless gesture, Vicky ran her hands across it, making Brick hiss as he flexed spastically, semen already leaking from his swollen cock to stain the front in a widening wet patch.

"Tell him what to do," Cain whispered.

Vicky glanced back at Cain, unsure what she was supposed to say.

"What would you do to him, if you could do anything?" Cain suggested. "Do that."

"Touch yourself," Vicky said eagerly. "Stroke your dick, but don't come."

Brick groaned, then pushed down his underwear, baring his thick cock. He began jerking his hand over the tip, massaging roughly as his buttocks flexed.

"Here, Vick," Cain whispered, handing Vicky the riding crop. "Use this."

Vicky shuddered as she took the crop, her sudden wet thatch betraying her excitement. She took a step forward, then turned and brought the crop down hard across Brick's tight bare ass. Brick grunted, then stroked himself faster, his movements straining.

"No, no," Cain said sternly, taking the crop from Vicky, and giving Brick a sharp rap on his furiously working hand. "Too fast, much too fast. Into the chair with you."

Vicky turned around to look at Cain, but Brick was already obediently moving, his penis bobbing as he went to a padded leather construct in the corner. Carefully, he stretched out across part of it, so that his frame was supported on his stomach, his arms to his sides, his hands gripping holds. His bare buttocks were exposed, his penis and balls through a hole in the front.

"Punish him," Cain said, handing Vicky the crop. "Ten strokes, at least. If he yells, begin again."

Vicky raised her hand with the crop, as Brick braced himself.

"Wait," Cain said quickly. Carefully, Cain pushed down Vicky's skirt, then helped her step out of it, the royal blue garters and stockings bright against her white skin. Then, he helped her remove her blouse, revealing the matching push up blue lace bra.

"There," Cain said approvingly. "Begin."

Vicky brought down her arm hard, the crop smacking into Brick's ass. He squirmed, but didn't make a sound. Nine times, Vicky brought the crop slapping down, reddening Brick's bottom, his grunts loud in the room.

Vicky paused, wanting badly to caress the muscular, reddened flesh.

"Give him what he truly wants," Cain said, taking the crop back. "Give him your hands. Punish, then pleasure." He reached up from behind, cupping her breasts to squeeze gently once, before he let her go, stepping back. "I know you want to touch him, Vic. Do it now."

With a shaky breath, Vicky reached down, and lightly swatted Brick with the flat of her palm. He grunted again, squirming. Emboldened, she brought down her hand again, the crack this time louder, more satisfying. Brick let out a cry, his hand clenching the grips of the chair, all his muscles taut.

Vicky slapped his firm, muscular buttocks again and again, watching the cheeks blush hotter and hotter, while Brick writhed and moaned. Finally, she could stand it no longer...her hands clenched Brick's ass, massaging and kneading. Then her fingers splayed possessively, the flesh hot under her hands. Still grasping one hard buttock in her left hand, Vicky reached around with her right and stroked Brick's hot cock, the bulging skin slippery with sweat and fluid. Then she spanked him again with her left hand, this time hard, her other hand stroking his penis fast, the flesh already beginning to vibrate as Brick approached orgasm.

Brick tensed, then jerked, yelling, his penis spurting come again and again, the thick white semen spattering on the carpet, the sharp scent filling the air. Vicky worked him rapidly in her hand, her other hand still massaging his ass between quick swats. Brick gasped, his ass muscles tensing once more, then slumped on the chair, breathing hard.

"Very good," Cain said approvingly. "You were masterful, Vicky. Now come here." He went to the bed, slipped on a condom, then beckoned to her.

Cain's skin was like silk in the dim light, his dark hair shadows. But his erection was easy to see, the stiff flesh waiting. Vicky patted Brick's ass lightly, then headed to Cain, eagerly sinking her body down on his, unable to contain a long groan as she was filled.

"Got you hot, spanking him," Cain murmured, his hands rising to lift and hold Vicky's breasts, positioning them so they were outside her bra, bared to him. "You're slick as a river, Vick."

Vicky closed her eyes and moved languidly, enjoying the sharp tugs at her nipples, the feeling of Cain's hard penis deep inside her. Then to her shock came the warm wetness of a mouth engulfing her left nipple. Her eyes shot open. Brick kneeled beside her, his mouth locked on her left breast, his other hand fondling her right one, stroking the soft skin as his mouth sucked hard, lips tightening around the nipple to tweak it.

Vicky let out a cry, her head going back in pure pleasurable sensation.

"Move up," Cain grunted. "Just watch yourself."

Brick straddled Cain, in back of Vicky, supporting his weight on his knees. His hands cupped each breast from behind, massaging and tugging at the nipples. "God, I'd love to clamp you," Cain breathed, kissing her shoulder, his tongue licking her neck.

Vicky stiffened slightly, unnerved. "What?"

"This, my darling," Cain said, producing a 12" long piece of black leather with loops on both ends. He fastened a loop around each of Vicky's nipples, and then tightened them down, each nipple reddening as it filled with blood. Then, Cain slipped his fingers under the leather thong and pulled slightly. Vicky yelped at the sudden stimulation, arching her back as she strove to move closer to Cain, following the leather.

"Just beautiful," Brick said appreciatively, cupping Vicky's breasts gently, his fingers rubbing her engorged, erect nipples. He moved around to her side and again suckled the left one in his mouth.

The wet and warm sensation was too much for Vicky, on top of constraints of the leather thong. She gasped, and jerked, her body contracting around Cain.

"Be a good girl," Cain purred. "Ride me, slow and sure."

Vicky groaned, then did as he asked, the sensation quickly overwhelming, her channel slick with juices, her orgasm building. But she knew better than to go against Cain. And why, when there was so much pleasure to be had in following his instructions?

Suddenly, Vicky was aware of Brick behind her, his hard body pressed to hers, his thick hard shaft trapped between her body and his, rubbing in time to Cain's thrusts inside her.

"You're so hot," she groaned, then leaned her head back, her head turning. "Please—"

Brick's mouth covered Vicky's his tongue plunging inside hers, tasting her. Vicky responded, her thrusts faster, seeking climax even as she took out all her desire on Brick, his kiss almost punishing in its passion.

There was a sharp whap! Brick straightened with a cry, tearing his mouth from Vicky.

"Remember yourselves," Cain said, not missing a stroke. He brandished the riding crop.

"I want her," Brick groaned, his pelvis pressing to Vicky's back, his erection throbbing. "I want to be inside her."

"She has to want you," Cain teased, laying aside the crop and grasping Vicky's hips. "She is in control of when you come, and how, Brick. Her wants are your commands."

"Please, Vicky," Brick said, kissing Vicky's shoulders and neck. "Please."

Vicky's lips opened. "Yes," Vicky breathed.

Brick groaned, then he moved back fast, carefully pulling on a condom, then smoothing on some Astroglide. Brick kneeled behind Vicky, positioning himself, then with a cry, he pushed in carefully, easing past Vicky's sphincter, his hard cock sliding deep into her.

Vicky shifted, suddenly uncomfortable. This hadn't been what she'd meant. Not only was she uncomfortable, but she was scared the strong man behind her would hurt her in pursuit of his orgasm. He was so much stronger than she was...

Vicky opened her mouth to protest and Brick drove in another inch, the sudden pinch enough to make Vicky gasp.

Cain had stopped moving, his eyes on Vicky as she groaned, squirming slightly as the feeling of being so full of flesh. He took her hands in his, squeezing gently. "You're safe, Vick," Cain said softly. "You're okay. Breathe."

"I'm nervous," Vicky managed. "I've never even thought—"

"That's why we're doing it," Cain replied, squeezing her hands again. "Most women don't imagine they would like this. And a good many men do not know how to control themselves. Brick does, or I'd not have let him lay a finger on you." Cain paused. "Will you trust me?"

Vicky was motionless, biting her lip as she stared down at Cain. His golden eyes were lustful, but also completely serious. She nodded, then stiffened slightly, bracing herself for what she was sure would be pain.

"Gently," Cain said, tapping Brick's ass with the crop. "This is all for her. You are not allowed to come yet."

Brick groaned, then began to pump steadily, his penis moving in and out by the smallest margin, stroking Vicky in a languid fashion. The movement impaled Vicky further on Cain's cock, her clit teased by his hard organ with every motion of Brick sliding home. To her amazement, an orgasm slowly built, but it felt like no other orgasm she'd had before. Instead of the orgasm originating from her clit, the sensation was building in her anus.

When Brick had entered her, the only thing Vicky had desired was for him to finish, so he'd get out of her. But this felt wonderful, each long stroke like a caress. Vicky groaned, her lips parting, sighs of pleasure each time Brick slipped deep inside. As the feeling built, Vicky pushed back against him, wanting him as deep as he could get, yearning for those last few strokes that would put her over the pinnacle and bring the orgasm crashing down on her like an avalanche.

The climax hit hard, Vicky's yell becoming a wild scream of pleasure as her sphincter tightened down on Brick, her anus spasming around his organ. As her orgasm ebbed, Brick gently slipped out, leaving Vicky breathless.

"Did you like it?" Cain purred, drawing Vicky down on his chest to hug, their bodies still connected.

"It felt so different," Vicky said, astonishment in her tone. "I didn't know that was possible. I always wondered why girls let guys do that to them—"

"Because it feels good," Brick said, kissing her cheek. He lay down beside Cain on his back, then removed the condom he wore, throwing it away. "There's no point to having exotic sex unless you and your partner enjoy it."

"And we all do," Cain said with surety, beginning to thrust. Vicky's moan was loud, surprise again in her tone as she felt the first stirrings of orgasm begin. Cain stroked rhythmically, each motion of his penis caressing her clit, teasing out her pleasure as the fire built within her. As she began to rock harder, pursuing her climax, Cain began to spank Vicky regularly, the slaps more playful than the normal discipline he offered. In an instant, Vicky was there, her body vibrating on Cain's, squeezing, and tightening around his stiffness. His cry matched hers as he thrust up suddenly, clutching her hips tight against his as he jerked and thrashed under her.

Panting, Vicky collapsed down on Cain, hugging him. Then Cain lifted her off him, moving her between him and Brick. For a few moments, no one spoke.

"It was so effortless," Vicky said finally, flushing slightly. "My orgasm, I mean. Why?"

"When you come being stimulated that way, it's easier to have another related orgasm right after," Brick supplied. "The trick is to be gentle, and to move the right way." He stroked Vicky's bare arm. "I'm glad I was able to give that to you, Vicky."

Vicky looked at him, unsure what to say. Then she smiled, telling herself she had no reason to be bashful or uptight when she was the most relaxed she had felt in weeks. "Thanks, Brick. I had no idea it would be like that."

"I'm glad you liked it, too," Cain said languidly, kissing Vicky's other arm. "I wasn't sure you would be open to the idea. I'm happy you were open to trying."

If everything Cain offered was this bliss-inducing, Vicky was open for anything. But she hesitated to voice that feeling, worried that she would sound too eager. All she could think about was how good she felt. And what was next? Something more for Brick, she was guessing. "But what about you?" Vicky said sultrily, taking Brick's half-hardened cock in her hand. She stroked slightly, pleased that the flesh began at once to fill out and stiffen. "You need to come—"

"Want to help me?" Brick said with a leer.

What Vicky wanted was to spread her legs and take that stiffness into her, and ride Brick until he burst. She moved to position his penis, so she could straddle him.

"In a moment," Cain said, hitting Vicky's hand lightly with the riding crop. "But Vic needs a little more time to recover, if she is going to have another good orgasm. And we want yours to be stunning too, Brick. Patience."

Vicky gritted her teeth, but stayed still. Cain would make good on his threat, if she disobeyed. She needed to hold back until it was time.

"You can't touch me," Brick teased Vicky. "But I can touch myself.' He stroked his penis slowly, the purple head disappearing again and again as he tugged at it, fluid leaking steadily from the tip, lubricating his manipulations.

Vicky watched him, getting hotter and hotter the longer she watched. Involuntarily she began to move, shifting in her eagerness.

"You want his cock, don't you?" Cain whispered in her ear. "You can have it, if you're good. But you need to do just what I say, Vick. We want to make this as good as we can for him."

All Vicky could think of was that flushed hard flesh, and how good it would feel as it slipped inside her. She nodded blindly, waiting for the word. Instead, she felt Cain's light touch on her thatch, then gentle rubbing. God, she was so wet she was dripping with desire, her clit swollen and protruding slightly in its eagerness to be touched. Cain slipped his fingers inside, making Vicky cry out in longing

"Condom."

Brick ripped open a foil packet, then slipped it on, smoothing the plastic down over his flesh.

"Remember, you are in control," Cain stated as he handed the crop to Vicky. "Make him work for his pleasure."

Crop in hand, Vicky eagerly moved to straddle Brick. Brick let out a groan as the thick head of his throbbing erection pushed into Vicky's wet folds.

She was so wet…and so tight! Brick pushed up, trying to go deeper. But Vicky raised herself, keeping only the tip of his penis inside her.

"Behave," she commanded, flicking him with the whip.

Two could play at that game. Brick withdrew slightly, rubbing her clit with the head of his dick. Vicky moaned, then rocked slightly, wetness seeping down over Brick's glistening organ, further lubricating his erection. Again and again Brick rubbed, stimulating Vicky until their cries were in tandem, their sexual organs slick.

"Please let me come," Brick groaned.

Vicky moaned, then pushed down hard, sliding Brick fully into her, the sweet feeling of being filled making her shudder. "No, not yet. Deep and slow."

"As you command." Brick stroked long and deep, holding Vicky's hips, his motion unhurried and deliberate.

The sensation was too much, the need for orgasm too base to resist for the couple. In seconds, their copulation degenerated into frenzied thrusting, both parties eager to come, lost in their desire.

The whip came down with a whap, striking Brick's chest. "Slower. She is first, always."

Vicky began to pant, her eyes closed. Brick resumed thrusting, deep, but also faster.

The climax came in a wave, Vicky's nails digging into Brick's chest, her cry of passion loud and long. Each new cry was punctuated by the slap of her buttocks with the flat of Brick's hand. As her climax ebbed, Brick rolled Vicky onto her back, then paused.

"I need it, bud."

"Of course," Cain said, instantly moving. "Hold still."

Brick went motionless, expectant. Then he felt the phallus edge past his sphincter muscle and relaxed, letting it in. In the space of a second, Brick was thrusting again, the heavy pressure building not only in his penis, but also his anus. Fluid leaked steadily from his penis, stimulating him within the condom, as Vicky's warm tightness stroked his shaft with each deep thrust. Brick let out an eager moan, then a loud "Yes!" as he felt his ass tighten around the dildo, his semen shooting again and again as his balls contracted in the intensity of double orgasm.

As Brick lay gasping, Cain gently removed the phallus, then took it into the bathroom. The sound of water running followed.

Vicky looked up at Brick, not sure what to say. He removed the condom, then wiped himself off with a tissue, his muscles flexing as he tossed it into the wastebasket.

"I needed it," Brick said with a relaxed smile. "You were perfect, Vicky. You might be new at this, but your actions were spot on. I loved how you teased me. That made it so much stronger when I came."

Cain returned, then lay down on the other side of Vicky. He caught her look of introspection, then chuckled. "You're wondering why I didn't use my own organ," he said, amused. "The answer is that neither of us are gay, Vick. Brick just likes anal orgasms sometimes. I'm happy to help him achieve them. But I have to be true to my own desires, which lie only with the female form."

Vicky nodded, flushing slightly.

"I know it probably sounds strange," Brick added. "I thought it was strange when Cain first suggested it—"

"I think your exact words were 'I don't fucking think so,'" Cain quipped.

The threesome laughed, the uneasy tension Vicky had been feeling slipping away with the humor

"Okay, you're right," Brick admitted. "I was worried you were gay, and that you'd gotten me back here planning to seduce me."

"Maybe into trying new things," Cain replied easily. "But not into being someone you aren't."

"So how did you first do it?" Vicky ventured, curious. "If Brick wasn't into it, I mean?"

"The way we did tonight, with you," Cain answered, hugging her. "Gentleness and precision are just as important in bed as passion and longing. Brick let me know what felt good to him, and how far he wanted to go. I respected those lines." He kissed her cheek.

"I'm just glad I was open-minded," Brick said, sheepish. "I love feeling so relaxed afterward."

Vicky stretched, searching herself for how she felt about what they had done. She was super relaxed, almost sleepy. Yes, her body ached slightly, but nothing hurt. "I'm glad I was, too. I'd never have asked for you to do that to me. I'd have been too embarrassed—"

"When you are here, you don't have to pretend," Cain said, squeezing Vicky in his arms. "I want to give you anything you need to feel satisfied. There is no judgment."

"We've only just scratched the surface," Brick murmured, shifting on the bed as he stretched his arms over his head. "That's the best part of these sessions of Cain's, discovering new pleasures."

Vicky stared, captivated by the ripple of Brick's muscles as he moved. She resisted the urge to reach out and caress his chest, then told herself indulging in desires was what she was here for. She rubbed Brick's chest with her left hand, marveling at the solid muscle, the thrill arousing her even in her satiated state.

"Ahh," Brick said, closing his eyes and smiling. "Yes, touch me. I loved to be touched."

"And I love to touch," Cain purred in Vicky's ear, cupping her bottom as he began kissing up her neck lightly. "I want to make all your fantasies reality, Vicky."

That's good, thought Vicky blissfully. The only problem is what do I ask for next? "I'm new to this," she said. "I'm not sure what to ask for next, though. My fantasies only ever went to two men."

Brick took her hand, gently kissing the back of it. "Then you need some new fantasies, Vicky." His blue eyes looked up at her teasingly. "I'd love to help you with that any night you're free."

"I'll take you up on that," Vicky purred right back, then she looked over her shoulder at Cain guiltily, wondering if she should have kept quiet.

Cain smiled, then bit her earlobe. "If I were a jealous man, Vic, I wouldn't have introduced you to Brick. I want you to discover all sources of pleasure. I intended for Brick to help in that journey, if tonight went well."

Vicky nodded eagerly, pushing aside the weak pleas of her moral upbringing. "Yes. I want that."

Brick smiled, then moved closer, hugging Vicky close. Being enfolded in his strong arms made her feel both small, and very safe. "Good," he whispered.

The three were quiet for a few moments, then Cain spoke up. "Do you have any friends who would be open to this kind of fun, Vicky? A friend you would feel comfortable sharing this newfound part of yourself with?"

Vicky shifted, running her hand through her hair as she sifted through a mental list of friends. "Maybe one," she said finally. "But I'm afraid it wouldn't work."

"Why not?" Cain said, his golden eyes bemused.

It wouldn't work because Vicky's friend Candy wasn't into really buff men like Brick; she favored tall, dark, and handsome, as Cain was. And there was no way Vicky was sharing Cain with Candy, even if Cain was willing to share her with his friends. But Vicky was not going to say any of that. "She likes blonde men who don't have a lot of muscle," Vicky said apologetically. "But I'm not sure that she would be into this anyway."

"Hmm," Cain said thoughtfully. "I think I can accommodate your friend's request with the help of an old friend. I'll make a call tonight."

Vicky's mouth fell open in shock. Cain was going to invite another man to join her and her friend? What had she gotten into?

"What about me?" Brick said grumpily. "I hope you both have some time in the next week to let me join in one night. I was feeling good, and now I'm feeling left out."

Both Vicky and Cain began talking at once, then with a smile and a look at one another, Cain motioned for Vicky to speak first.

"Yes, there is going to be another night, and it's going to be next week," Vicky assured Brick, running her hand again over his chest. "And the week after that, and the one after that, if you're up for it."

Brick leered, then cupped her face with his hand. He leaned in carefully, and gave Vicky a long slow kiss. "Yes," he said happily. "Just say the word and I'm here...or there... or wherever you want me."

Vicky felt a rush of power. She kissed Brick back, slipping her tongue into his mouth. He responded, pulling her out of Cain's arms to straddle his waist, his erection already firming beneath her buttocks.

Cain watched them, pushing down his slight sadness. Many times when he had brought together friends in sessions, not only had sparks flown of the sexual variety, but also of the romantic variety. Often that had led to the couple deciding on exclusivity...and him being the one left out. But for now, Vicky still had a lot to experience. He was going to enjoy this time with her, no matter how long it lasted.

THE END

THREE STRIKES

TARA FOX HALL

Candy rolled her eyes when Vicky invited her to dinner to meet her new boyfriend, Cain, especially when the offer included not only voyeurism as dessert, but also a partner for her to join in the fun. No man had ever been able to give Candy real pleasure, no matter what sex toys they had tried. But Cain's friend Devlin is not a man; he's a centuries old vampire who's more than up to the challenge, and willing to do whatever it takes to give Candy what she's been missing.

THREE STRIKES

Candy lounged back in her Jacuzzi bath, letting her tired muscles relax. Unbidden, thoughts of the night filled her mind, the images upsetting her all over again.

Randy had been great all through dinner, just as charming as he'd been on their other previous dates, conscientious and caring. His brown eyes had been so warm, so loving. She'd decided over dessert that tonight was the night.

She'd suggested they go back to his place. Randy had lived up to his name, eagerly accepting. They'd kissed, the chemistry that had been present since their first meeting heating her body up until it felt on fire. When the clothes had come off, he'd been every bit the stud, his penis already swollen. He'd felt so good inside her, moving rapidly, his murmuring possessive and lustful.

Then, it had happened again, just like it always had before.

Candy had loved the movement of his body on hers, but the climax wouldn't start, no matter how Randy moved, or how she'd positioned herself. And he'd done his damnedest. But while the sex had been enjoyable at first, the longer it went on and she didn't come, the more agitated he became, his soft murmuring changing to encouragement, then almost demand. And Candy had done what she'd always done before; she'd faked it.

Randy hadn't guessed. He'd held her close, and kissed her, then come himself. After he'd hugged her, telling her how happy he was that he'd made her happy. It had been unbearable. But luck was on her side, as he'd fallen asleep soon after. While he was snoring, she'd snuck out carefully, giving his sexy sleeping visage a sight of reluctant farewell. But what other choice was there?

The worst thing was knowing that he'd tried so hard. But so had all the others, over the years. Even her ex-husband, Mark, had tried hard, experimenting with all kinds of different condoms, gadgets, and porn videos. Some had been enjoyable, others laughable. But in the end, he'd given up. He'd left her after two years for a stripper named Vixen who no doubt came at the drop of a hat.

Why couldn't she be normal, like other women? Women came all the time with men, no problem, and there were all kinds of instruction videos, and such. There was one bright spot; at least she knew she could come. The problem was she couldn't come with anyone else. All her orgasms her entire life had been through masturbation. Which was why she was in the Jacuzzi at three in the morning. After being stimulated for so long by Randy with no release, she'd never be able to sleep. It was time to take care of business.

Candy leaned back, her elegant hand rotating the silvery jet nozzle, angling it perfectly so that the gentle stream ran over her clitoris. Instantly, her arousal rose up, that wanting for more turning to desire, then demand. She arched up her pelvis, moving a hair's breadth closer.

Too close was too hard, like some of the men had been over the years. And too far was like Mark had been, giving not nearly enough stimulation.

The pleasurable feeling built slowly, the hot bathwater making sweat bead on her large breasts. Her skin flushed, then darkened, her lips parting gently.

God, this felt so wonderful!

Candy sighed, then adjusted the knob slightly, turning it just a tad stronger. Abruptly the tingling pleasure turned to pure joy, her climax slowly tightening within her, her muscles tense with anticipation, her breaths coming faster.

Her hips began to move slowing underwater, striving for more stimulation, eager to push the water deeper. The need to come was now unbearable, to be so close and yet not there! This was how she'd felt all tonight! She needed to come. She needed to come now!

She grasped the edge of the tub tightly, moving herself frantically in the water, panting hard, her eyes closed, her head moving wildly as she sought satisfaction. Suddenly she was there, the orgasm flooding her senses, her scream deafening. Candy thrust slow and rhythmically, her grunts coarse and base, each cry ripping out of her as the feeling she'd sought for so long washed over her.

Breathing hard, Candy eased back into the water, her shoulders slumping in relief, spent. God, that had been good. But now, she was way too hot...

She ran cold water into the tub, splashing some of the icy water on her face. A little trickled down, making her gasp as her nipples reflexively tightened. She cupped some water from the tap, then drank it, taking another handful to smear on her sweaty face.

The phone rang.

Who the hell was that this time of night? Randy? Well whomever it was would just have to leave a message. She eased back in the water, blissful.

The phone continued to ring, then gave up, the answering machine clicking on.

Candy considered her options. Should she try for another? She still felt randy. Snorting at her unintended pun, she again moved close to the jet, getting herself into position. She'd just begun to feel the first delicious stirrings when the damn phone began ringing again.

She tried to ignore it, but the jarring ring broke her concentration, the orgasm slipping away to be replaced by irritation. Swearing, Candy got out of the tub, water splashing over the edge, and stalked to the phone naked, water dripping off her.

Her finger jabbed at the intercom button. "What?" she demanded.

"You won't believe this, Can!" the female voice said excitedly. "I've had the most incredible night—"

And I had one like all the rest; unfulfilling, Candy thought grumpily. But you've got to be nice, Vicky's your best friend. "That's wonderful, Vicky. I'm happy for you—"

"I want you to meet him," Vicky gushed. "Are you busy tomorrow night?"

"No," Candy said slowly. "But are you sure he's ready for a meet and greet?"

"Actually...it's not a meet and greet," Vicky said, very uncomfortable. "I wanted to ask you a favor."

This was odd. Vicky was rarely uncomfortable about anything. She had no trouble walking into adult bookstores, or ordering all sorts of things online. "What is it?"

"Are you...would you like to...are you interested in watching?"

"I'm guessing you aren't asking me to a movie with your new guy," Candy said slowly, appalled. "What in the world made you choose me as a person to ask?"

"You're my best friend," Vicky replied. "I'd feel most comfortable if it was you. The guy's name is Cain, and he's into a lot of new things he wants me to try—"

"Then are you sure you aren't just doing them for him?" Candy asked pointedly. "This isn't like you, Vicky."

"It's not," Vicky said, then laughed. "But I love it. I love what he does to me, how he makes me feel. You wouldn't believe how good it was tonight with him and...oh, Candy, I thought my head was going to explode—"

Candy grimaced, trying to control her jealousy. "Vicky, I'm supportive of you, you know that. But honestly, I'm not into just watching you and him get your rocks off—"

"There will be someone there for you, Can," Vicky said abruptly. "Cain guaranteed you'd like him, and that he'd fulfill all your fantasies."

"Oh, really?" Candy challenged. "Fine, then. I want to meet this Cain. But be prepared I might just deck him and walk out, Vicky. And don't call me Can. You know I never liked it when Mark used to do that, either."

"Sorry, Candy," Vicky apologized. "So, can I pick you up tomorrow at seven?"

"Sure," Candy said. "I'll be waiting."

<hr />

That next evening, both of the women stood at Cain's door, expectant.

"This is a gorgeous place," Candy said, taking in the extensive landscaping, the beautiful stately and sprawling house. "Even the door is beautiful. Is that a sunrise in the stained glass?"

"A sunset," Vicky whispered back, poised to knock. "He said he loves sunsets."

The door opened before the first knock fell, the large oak door swinging wide. Cain stood there, his expression eager, a devil-may-care smile on his handsome features. Candy drank him in, all of her righteous plans evaporating like mist under those cool golden eyes.

"So this is the lovely Candy," Cain said seductively, taking her hand gently, and raising it to his lips. "I'm pleased to make your acquaintance. I'm glad you agreed to join us tonight." He smiled. "I hope it will be the first night of many."

Fat chance, Candy thought, smiling outwardly. "It's good to meet you, Cain."

"Please come in," Cain said, moving to Vicky and taking her hand. "Dinner's about to be served." He kissed her hand, gave her a smoky look, and walked through a doorway. "This way, ladies."

Candy shot Vicky a surprised look. Vicky made a face back that said she was surprised, too, as they both followed Cain down a long hall.

Cain led them into the dining room. "Please, sit down."

The table was set for three, the cut glass wineglasses full. A large bouquet of red and white roses was on the table, their soft luxurious scent wafting through the air.

"These are beautiful," Vicky said, smelling them deeply. "But where is your friend, Cain?"

"He will be here after dinner," Cain said, smiling pleasantly. "Don't worry. He wouldn't miss this, Vicky." He indicated the empty chairs. "Please sit down."

At least she'd get some dinner out of this, Candy thought grumpily as she sat. The friend was obviously a no-show.

When they were seated, Cain clapped his hands. In walked two serving girls, one dark, one light, their attire perfect little French maids, festooned with black and white lace, their hair upswept under small caps with a few curls dangling, their scoop necks revealing silky breasts, and their legs in fishnet stockings with stiletto heels. Silently, they began to bring in the dishes, serving them. There were many dishes and several courses; various breads, brie and crackers, then a savory pasta with sauce of fresh tomatoes and herbs.

The food was delectable, each mouthful fresh and delightful to Candy's taste buds. She ate heartily, not caring if her jeans were stretching. No one else was coming, so why pass up good food?

The serving girls took away each dish as the threesome finished, then began bringing in some kind of dessert, a large chocolate confection. As the dark girl set it down, she jostled Vicky's wineglass, a bit of wine slopping over the edge.

"Yvette," Cain said sharply.

Yvette quickly moved back, hanging her head. "I'm sorry, sir."

"I know you are," Cain said lovingly. "But you know what has to happen now." He motioned to the lighter skinned girl. "Chianti? Would you please serve?"

Chianti nodded, then went to Yvette, leading her to Cain. She released Yvette's arm and began to serve the dessert. Candy and Vicky barely noticed her, all their attention on Cain.

Yvette carefully lay face down across Cain's lap, trembling slightly. He rested his hand on her lower back, gently stroking, then reached to her skirts, yanking them upwards to reveal her dusky cheeks, the black thong between them accentuating the round firm muscle. He paused, his eyes glancing up to meet Vicky and Candy's riveted faces.

"Please finish your cake," he said, the corner of his mouth curling up just a little. "I'll just need a minute."

His arm came down, the slap of his hand delivering a sharp crack to Yvette's ass. Yvette stiffened, a low moan coming from her throat as she squirmed slightly.

Vicky gave a sharp intake of breath. Candy looked at her. Vicky's heaving chest, her rapt expression, the way her hands were clenching her napkin in her fist made it evident she was into this. Flushing, Candy focused on her dessert, eating bite after bite, the rhythmic cracks regular, even as the moaning intensified. Just as she finished and prepared to head for the door with a quick excuse, Yvette gave a sharp cry, then slumped on Cain's lap, gasping.

Carefully, Cain stood, helping Yvette to stand. Chianti came to Yvette's side, and held her around the waist.

"Thank you," Yvette murmured to Cain, her full lips slack with satisfaction.

"It's my turn next time," Chianti said poutingly, then kissed Yvette's cheek. "Come with me, my pet." She led the dark woman out, her arm slipping down to rest on the dark woman's behind, rubbing possessively.

This was too weird, Candy thought. *I'm out.*

She got to her feet. "Thank you for the dinner, Cain, and it was good to meet you. But I really have to be going—"

"Are you sure?" Cain said, taking Vicky's hand. "We're just ready to begin, Candy. I'm sure my friend will be here soon. He is always prompt."

Whatever. "No, thank you." She turned to Vicky. "Give me a call tomorrow."

Vicky blinked her eyes, ripping them away from Cain's with effort. "What?

Sure, Candy. Tomorrow. Thanks for coming." She turned back, taking Cain's hand. Cain led her out of the room, then up a large staircase.

Well, that was nice. Vicky was going to get an earful later. Candy grabbed her purse, then strode out of the dining room to the front door. She put her hand on the knob, relieved, and also crestfallen that a night that had held such promise had turned out to be a dud.

"Leaving so soon?" a sexy voice asked. "What a disappointment."

Candy turned. Gliding toward her—there was no other word for how gracefully he moved—was a man who looked enough like Cain to be his twin brother down to his golden eyes. But where Cain had dark hair, and his skin was tanned, this man had pale skin and golden blonde hair. Stubble dotted his cheeks, the fair hair glinting in the dim light. He was dressed casually in jeans and a white shirt.

This was Cain's friend? Wow. "You missed dinner."

The man took her hand, kissing it. Oddly, his lips and hand were cool, not hot. "I had other arrangements, my dear. Was the meal good?"

"Wonderful," Candy said, trying to control her racing heart. "The dessert was some kind of luscious cake." She smiled self-depreciatingly. "I shouldn't have eaten so much."

"On the contrary, dessert should be enjoyed by whatever means it can be procured," the man said, smiling. "I am Dev. And you are?"

"Candy. I'm Vicky's friend."

"Cain is my friend, too, a good one now for many years," Dev said, taking Candy's hand. "Come. We are expected upstairs."

All of her reservations had melted in the heat of his tone, and the desire that was already raging through her. Candy took his hand, letting herself be led upstairs, her thoughts consumed by what Dev would look like without his clothes, and how the intense undercurrent that ran through all his words would manifest itself in action.

"Are you related to Cain?" Candy asked, as they approached the half-open bedroom door.

"Yes, but distantly," Devlin said, one side of his mouth smiling slightly, in just the same way Cain had during dinner. "Come. We may be in time for the climax."

They entered the room just in time to see Vicky sink down on Cain's engorged shaft, the thick glistening head sliding inside her as she positioned herself astride him. Dev grabbed Candy's hand, pulling her onto a large settee that faced the bed, her behind resting in his lap, his arms around her.

Cain held Vicky above him, his penis clearly visible between her thighs. The he began to move, thrusting up slowly over and over, just the tip sheathing itself in Vicky, rubbing her clitoris over and over each time it sank in. Vicky moaned repeatedly with each thrust, the sound fraught with desperation as the moments ticked by. Suddenly, Vicky began moving fast, throwing her head back in a cry of sheer lust as she took him fully inside.

There was a sharp crack, and a startled cry from Vicky. Candy's eyes went wide. Cain had spanked Vicky just as he'd spanked Yvette downstairs.

"No," Cain said firmly, pushing Vicky up from him slightly with his hands, so again only the tip of his penis was within her. "Now we must begin again—"

"Please, no," Vicky breathed, arching her back, her hips flexing in vain as she tried to take him back inside. "Please, I need it so bad—"

"I know," Cain said, lust coloring his tone in shades of aching desire. He leaned upwards, teasing her nipples with his mouth; first one dusky areole, then the other. Vicky let out another cry, and tried to grab him, even as he held her hands in his, spreading them wide before he pushed them down to the bed. With a soft metallic click, he fastened both of Vicky's hands in handcuffs.

Candy stared, riveted, mouth agape.

"On your knees," Cain instructed, using his hands to spread Vicky's legs, moving her up from his penis slightly with his hands, even as the tip stayed inside her. Then he carefully began to move her hips toward his, teasing her with his penis, stroking as Vicky swayed and jerked on her knees.

"Please," Vicky panted, her eyes beseeching Cain. "Deeper, please…"

"All in good time," Cain said, then took a nipple in each hand, rubbing the red, taut nub hard between his fingers. Vicky shuddered, then cried out again, almost crazed.

"I love to watch you like this," Cain said hungrily, his thrusts deliberate and slow, each motion of his cock stroking Vicky's labia. "I love how wild you get—"

"Come," Dev whispered, standing and leading Candy from the room. Bewildered, she followed him, casting a last longing look at Vicky and Cain as Dev shut the door behind them. Dev took her down the hall, then to the last room.

"Why couldn't we stay?" Candy asked, flushing, as Devlin brought her into the room, and shut the door behind them. "I wanted to see the finale."

"Did you?" Dev said, locking the door and turning to face her, his expression knowing. "Would you not rather have a finale of your own, if not several?"

Candy looked away, flushing.

Dev moved closer, his graceful walk like a panther's stalk. "You haven't ever, have you? Tell me the truth."

Candy looked up at him, then away, not wanting to admit her secret.

"We left because your friend Vicky clearly has more than a little discipline yet to undergo," Dev said with a bemused smile. "Cain and she must have just begun their love affair, to have her so rough around the edges."

Irked instantly at his comment, Candy lost her shyness, her head coming up, her flashing brown eyes locking on those cool golden ones. "If he's going to hurt her, you tell me now, Dev. Does he have someone else?"

"That is between Vicky and Cain," Dev said, his manner oddly comforting. "They are both adults and can make decisions as such." He clasped Candy's hand in his, giving it a slight squeeze before releasing his grip. "But he's not married or engaged, no. And neither am I, which I'm sure would be your next question."

Candy flushed, torn between whether to protest that casual sex—especially exotic stuff—wasn't for her and wanting to admit that she was single, too. "I'm not in the habit of having sex with someone I just met. I don't know you at all."

"The question is do you want to know me," Dev corrected gently, rubbing his stubbled cheek on her smooth cheek. He moved back, then grinned. "I would like to know every curve of you, Candy, and see if you taste as good as your name."

No one had ever said anything like this to her before, not since her high school boyfriend's lame attempts at seduction. But there was nothing amateur about Dev. His attitude, tone, and bearing was completely confident.

"We can be lovers tonight, if you wish," Dev offered, his hand touching her face lightly before sliding down over Candy's neck and chest. "And I give you my word that if you do as I ask, I can give you your own...culmination."

The word wasn't one Candy would have described as erotic, but it sent thrills singing through her body. Dev's voice rang with surety. The others she had known...they had been boys with intent, but little expertise. Here was a master, a man who clearly had the skill to make her moan with passion in his arms. If anyone could give her an orgasm with his penis in this life, it was this god of a man.

"What…what would you want me to do?" she asked tentatively.

"Anything I ask you to," Dev replied, flashing a devilish smile. "Be assured I wouldn't ask for anything out of the norm for myself. But I have an inkling that you may need something exotic." He put his hands on her arms, his cool skin against hers bringing goose bumps, even as his lips gently kissed up the side of her throat. "I know how turned on you were in there, watching. We can have that same scenario here, if you wish. I led you to this room because I know it has everything you could want—"

He leaned in closer, his arms going around her, his hands sliding down to cup her rear, bringing her hips tight to his. Candy drew a sharp intake of breath as Dev gently thrust his hard penis against her, the whisper of the cloth barrier of their clothes no impediment to his throbbing masculinity.

"—including me."

Candy's heart was racing. She believed him, but could she trust him? "I'd need a safe word."

"No safe word," Dev said gently. "This is not my fantasy, it's yours, Candy."

God, she had to say the right thing. What should she ask? "What…what is your safe word?"

"You have permission to do anything you need, my blushing temptress," Dev whispered, then his lips nibbled her earlobe. "We'll begin with your fantasy. What you ask for will lead us to the end." He kissed her hand, then flicked his eyes up to lock on hers. "Do you consent?"

There was no other choice. She could never leave this room now, not without knowing if Dev could do it. "Yes," Candy said raggedly. She began undoing Dev's shirt. "Please, just kiss me—"

Dev cut off her words in a ravishing kiss, his arms grasping her tightly. Candy's movements were frantic as she stripped off Dev's shirt, then her own clothes.

Dev watched her, nodding appreciatively. "A bold woman is something to be admired." He kissed her again, then smiled. "Direct me, my temptress."

Candy looked at the bed. Maybe later. If this was her fantasy, she wanted it all. She gestured to the velvet antique lounge chair, patting the blood red cushion. "There. Please take off your pants and sit there."

Dev nodded once, then did as she asked, his large penis coming free of his clothes. He reclined back on the lounge, his stiff Johnson standing proudly.

Candy went to her knees, grasping it with her hands, one hand clutching it possessively, the other stroking the tip in her fist. Dev groaned, then flexed, his penis moving in her hand eagerly. Candy dipped her head, taking the swollen head in her mouth, the tight firm flesh smooth against her tongue as she licked and sucked, teasing the small cleft with her tongue. Dev groaned, then rested his hand on her head, stroking her hair as she massaged his length, slipping more and more of the shaft into her throat.

Candy played with Dev for a good five minutes, until she could feel her own sex was slippery wet, and his breathing was fast. Carefully, she let him slip from her mouth, then settled astride him, eagerly accepting Dev's hard cock as it slipped inside her inch by precious inch.

"You like that," Dev purred, his lips again at Candy's throat as he began thrusting slow and deliberately. "But you need more, don't you? This is diverting, but not exciting to you, not in the way it should be."

"Please," Candy asked, her lips devouring Dev's chest, his neck, his face. "I love how you feel, but—"

"Hold still," Dev said, stopping his gentle motion. Carefully, he picked up Candy and brought her still impaled to the bed, easing her down as he rolled carefully onto his back. As Cain had with Vicky, Dev brought out some handcuffs, clamping each leather bracelet around Candy's wrist.

Instantly, Candy felt her heart quicken. She looked down at Devlin, curious to see him with some metal clips attached by a chain. "What are those?"

"Nipple clamps," he said. "Hold still."

Candy let out a yelp as he affixed one to her nipple. The sensation was pressure just this side of pain. "Hey, wait, I don't—"

Dev affixed the other one, Candy's second yelp stopping her words.

"There," Dev said approvingly. He grasped the chain, giving it a tug towards him. Candy let out a gasp, leaning forward quickly on her knees to alleviate the pressure on her nipples. Suddenly scared, she looked down at the stranger below her, her chest heaving.

"Shh," Dev said, kissing first one clamped nipple, then the other. Candy let out a hiss of pleasure, even as she watched him alertly.

Devlin began to move again below her, each stroke unhurried. Candy's tenseness left her slowly, the languid pleasure building with each wet stroke.

But as before, the climax did not begin, even as her body became slick with sweat and her secretions. Angry and upset, she stopped moving, opening her mouth to tell Dev it was useless.

"Shh," Dev said chidingly, putting a finger to her lips. "We have only just begun, Candy. And I am enjoying this journey with you immensely. Trust me. I'll not let you down."

"I just can't take the pressure," Candy whispered, upset. "Why can't it just happen?"

"Because you are special," Dev said fondly, tweaking the chain again so Candy gasped again. He reached beside the bed, then produced a blindfold. "Lean closer."

Candy shrugged, then leaned down, resigned. Yet instead of Dev putting the blindfold on her, he put it on himself, using her loosely chained hands to smooth it down over his eyes.

The moment his eyes left her, Candy felt as if a weight had lifted. She looked down at Dev below her, relishing his apparent helplessness. He did not speak, his lips slightly parted.

At once, a wild need rose in her. Candy unclasped the chains from her wrists, and clamped them onto Dev's wrists. Then she slid him fully inside, this time to the hilt. Dev's mouth went slack, his groan loud in the room as Candy rode him, her body straining on his.

"Deeper," she said gutturally. "I want you buried in me, Dev. When you come, I want you as deep as possible. Possess me!"

"You are mine," Dev growled, grasping her hips with his hands, and moving her fast, the friction of their two bodies frantic with need.

All at once, Candy felt it; the elusive climax finally appearing as if by a miracle, the burgeoning feeling widening and growing until it was undeniable, the crest close enough to touch. Maddened, she reached down and grasped Dev's balls, squeezing firmly. Dev bucked beneath her, the sensation and stimulation ripping wide the orgasm. Candy screamed loud and long, each wail of release echoing in the large room. Devlin shouted, his hands holding her hips prisoner as he delved inside again and again, shuddering as he spent himself.

Candy clutched Dev close, her naked body trembling, her breath coming in sharp pants. Carefully, Dev reached up and removed the blindfold over his eyes. With a careful deft touch, he removed the clamps, the release of pressure bringing a sharp cry from Candy as blood flowed back into her throbbing, reddened nipples.

Dev cupped her breasts, massaging the nipples gently. "Sore?"

Candy nodded, wincing.

Dev continued to massage, and over a minute or two, the throbbing subsided to tenderness. He brought her down to lie beside him, then he gently kissed her mouth, her cheeks and forehead.

"Thank you," she said with a sigh.

"You're welcome," Dev said fondly. "You are a complex lover, Candy. You want both to dominate, and be dominated. Achieving your balance between the two is the key, as both are necessary for your total satisfaction."

He was right, damn it. All the men before had done all kinds of things to her to excite her, and tried all kinds of toys on her. But they had never let her do anything to them. No one had even suggested it, until Dev.

Dev moved her off him gently, jerking slightly as her body unjoined from his. He settled her next to him, slipping his arm around her shoulders then kissed her forehead gently.

"There is nothing more satisfying than that surprised look of wonderment and peace you wear," Dev whispered tenderly. "I'm pleased that I could be the one to give you that, Candy."

"I am, too," she whispered back, her chest still heaving. "I didn't think I could."

"Of course you can, Candy," Dev replied, shifting slightly beside her. "Perhaps I should call you Can."

"Don't you dare," Candy warned him, but her tone was so relaxed, her words slurred slightly, then became a yawn.

"Rest," Dev ordered, stretching his arms above his head, one arm covering his eyes.

Emboldened by his prone nakedness, Candy rolled closer, kissing up his chest of golden down, her hands sliding down his taut stomach to rest on one lean thigh.

Dev uncovered his eyes and looked down at her, that bemused expression back on his face. "Ready again so soon? I'd thought you'd want some time to recover."

Candy moved back slightly, her boldness instantly replaced by nervousness. "I...I, um..."

"What is it?" Dev said, resting one long fingered hand on her smooth back, rubbing gently. "Tell me. There is nothing you could say that would surprise me."

Just say it. If you don't say it, you might never feel this way again, Candy thought hurriedly. Her words tumbled from her lips before she could stop them. "I just didn't want you to leave, um…now that we're done."

"And who says we are done?" Dev said innocently, then laughed, the rich luxuriant sound caressing Candy, moving her desire to stir in her loins, even sated as she was. "Not I. Or did you want to end here, now?"

"No," Candy said more hesitantly. "But I thought you might."

"Who were these cads who acted so coarsely with you," Dev said, a thread of disgust in his words, even as he hugged her close to him. "No man of quality loves a woman and leaves her like a discarded handkerchief once used." He kissed her lips gently, then moved to the side of her throat, still kissing. "I am not leading you to sleep in an effort to slip away unnoticed. I will leave in the early dawn, not before. But you are no doubt tender from our lovemaking, Candy." He kissed harder, and Candy felt the pressure of teeth, then a gentle prick as he nipped her skin with his incisors. "And I want to experience our next time as this one began, with you eager, not still sated with faint echoes of climax."

Candy wasn't sure how to respond. There was something odd about Dev, about the way he talked, and some of the words he chose. That he was enjoying teaching her was a given, but why did he enjoy it so much? Most exciting; what would they do next?

Deciding that last was the answer she needed most, Candy nestled into Dev, shoulder, and closed her eyes. She was asleep in moments

---

When Candy awoke, she was alone in bed. At once, despair rose up in her, and she sat up quickly. But Dev was just on the settee where they had first joined, looking into the fire. Curious, Candy got up from the bed, and walked over, sitting at his feet.

"Subservient in satiation?" Dev said, with a pleased smile. "Or did you wish to make love before the fire?"

"What do you want?" Candy replied. "What is your fantasy?"

Dev's face closed off for a second, as if a shadow had passed over it, then he smiled faintly. "To lose myself in you, tonight, Candy. To just be here."

There was a sadness about his words that detracted from their impact. "How can you," Candy countered. "When you aren't here, but somewhere else?"

She expected him to be angry, or to deny it, but Dev shrugged. "I have been reliving old memories, my dear. But—" he pulled her up to sit next to him "—now that you are awake, I'm more than happy to leave that dread behind for more pleasurable memories. Let us waste no more time on past evil, when there is so little night left."

There was so much Candy wanted to ask, like the name of the woman he'd been hurt by, or what had happened. But he likely wouldn't tell her, either way. And selfishly, Candy wanted more orgasms. Later would be soon enough to hear Dev's story.

"Yes, before the fire," she said huskily, lying down on her back, beckoning to him.

Devlin smiled, then lowered himself down with supple grace, grasping her and pulling her close, his lips seeking hers eagerly. That first taste was heady, his tongue licking her top lip, as he suckled her bottom one, then thrusting again deep. His erection was already pushing against her inner thigh insistently, demanding entrance into her warm wetness as he moved atop her. Spreading her legs wide, he moved between then, then supported his weight on his hands, teasing her wet folds with his hard cock, just the tip entering and withdrawing, as Cain had done to Vicky.

But Candy was not about to be denied. Her torso arched up and her hands reached around, clasping Dev's hard buttocks, and pulled him forward, sliding him all the way in to the hilt. There was a slight pain, but the pleasure steamrolled it, making Candy's hips immediately begin to move as Devlin began kissing her throat.

After their first time, Candy expected the orgasm to come much easier. Yet again it was elusive, the pleasure of his hard penis inside her undeniable, yet unfulfilling.

Devlin paused, then withdrew from her body with such speed Candy jerked. Before she could react, Dev flipped her onto her stomach, and spread her legs wide, cupping her womanhood in his hand. Deftly, a finger penetrated her, then stroked her swollen nub. Candy writhed and cried out, the sensation too much to handle.

"You be a good girl," Devlin whispered in her ear, his voice oddly scary. "Or I'll have to spank your fine ass."

His words were coarse, the most offensive he'd uttered. Yet Candy's arousal raised a notch, even as she continued to writhe under his probing hand.

"Hold still and take it," Dev whispered throatily. "Or your virgin white cheeks are going to be red as that settee cushion before we're through."

"Stop," Candy breathed, still wriggling. "Please, I—"

Dev's hand came down with a crack on her ass, bringing a yelp and a sharp sting. Candy paused, chest heaving, then began struggling wildly. Dev brought his hand down again, then again, each crack of his hand reddening her ass more, her smooth flesh beginning to swell with the repeated strikes.

"Stop," Candy cried, going limp. "I'll be good, I promise."

"Yes, you will," Dev purred, then moved his body atop hers, sliding his hard, glistening cock into her. He pushed in deeply, then began moving slightly, stimulating her clit and her vagina with deep, sure strokes.

Candy groaned.

"Tell me you like my cock in you," Dev purred. "Tell me you want it deeper."

"Yes, deeper," Candy moaned, grabbing fistfuls of carpet.

"Please—"

Devlin's hand moved beneath Candy, cupping her breasts, rubbing the nipples in time to his thrusts, then squeezing hard.

Candy let out a sharp cry of pleasure mixed with pain, then felt the first stirrings of orgasm.

Devlin let go of her breasts, his hands moving down to her lower belly. With a slight push, he moved her back as he thrust forward into her cunt, going deeper than he ever had before in his thrusts. There was a slight pain as he hit her cervix, then Candy went weak, the orgasm rising rapidly with each successive thrust, the scream tearing out of her as she came.

Devlin shouted, pumping frantically, then slowing as he finished coming. Carefully he withdrew, then rolled onto his back with a satisfied sigh.

Candy rolled onto her side, facing him, unsure what to say. Part of her wanted to accuse him of something, for how he'd just dominated her. The other part was still reeling from the amazing power of the orgasm.

"There may be blood," Dev said gently. "Because I went so deep."

Candy shivered, and he drew her close.

"You need a little pain to let yourself ride to climax," Dev continued. "While I'm happy to give you that, my dear, please be aware that some men will not restrain themselves. Choose your lovers wisely, so you do not end up hurt."

Crestfallen, Candy rolled onto her back, so she didn't look at him. It was easy to see by his words that this time, Dev was done with her. Hadn't she been good enough? What else could she have done that she hadn't? Maybe he'd wanted head? No, that couldn't be it…

Dev moved closer to her, propping himself up on one arm. "I can tell you're offended. I meant no offense in my warning. I just—"

"You basically told me to find other lovers," Candy said, her voice wavering between bitterness and tears.

Dev didn't reply.

"How can you say that to me?" she said, looking him full in the face, her tear-filled eyes searching his for some emotion, "Especially after what you just did to me?"

Devlin sighed, then smiled widely, revealing fangs.

Candy started, then tried to scuttle backward. Devlin reached out and grabbed her arm, pulling her close.

"No, you look," he said coldly. "This is what I am. Say it."

"Vampire," Candy breathed.

Dev nodded. "I have several lovers I take blood from, Candy. You could not be the only one, unless you want our relationship to last only a few weeks, and then die."

"Did you…drink my blood?"

"Just a taste, as you slept," Dev conceded. "You smelled free of disease, so I thought, 'what the hell'."

Candy blinked, trying to process it all.

"Your look says it all," Dev continued, laying back down on his back and staring into the flames. "Vampires are fine for the movies, or for fantasies. But when it's your blood you have to give up, the appeal is diminished."

Candy felt her throat. "I have no wounds, Dev. My skin is unbroken."

"Because I healed you, my dear."

Was he crazy? Dear God, she hoped not. But maybe she was, to even be considering some sort of arrangement. Candy took Dev's hand. "I want to see you again," she said. "If you need my blood, I'll give it to you. I'm assuming that you'd take only a little?"

Dev raised his eyebrows, then smiled. "Of course, my dear. But if you're asking if I'd require your blood in return for sex, the answer is no. I enjoy bringing you to climax, in and of itself. I would like to see you again, even if all we share is pleasure."

"I want to see you again," Candy said bluntly. "I…can we have a standing…um, date?"

"For sexplay?" Dev replied. "If you wish. But understand that I don't promise monogamy." He ran his hand down her smooth bare shoulder. "But I don't require it, either. You can come to me for as long as you wish, and I'll welcome you to my bed. When you choose to end this arrangement, I'll not be upset. And not—" he pulled her close forcefully, drawing a gasp from her throat "—because I won't miss you, Candy. Vampires have three strikes against us from the first. We don't age, we must have blood, and we have to avoid the sun." He kissed her throat, pricking her neck with his fangs. "We tend to make bad boyfriends."

"Maybe you do," Candy said, resolute. "But you've been the most considerate lover I've ever had. You're the first man to value my orgasm over your own. You're also the first man I ever met that wasn't scared of being dominated." She stretched, baring her throat completely. "I want this with you, if you want it with me. I want all of you."

Dev kissed Candy's throat, even as he shifted atop her. "Then let us consummate our arrangement, lover."

Devlin bore down with his hips, his large stiff penis sliding into her wet folds. Candy groaned, then clutched Dev close as he began to move.

"Now that I know what you need," Dev said gently. "I can help you get there."

Candy let herself drift on pleasurable sensation. But after only a few minutes, Devlin withdrew, then helped her stand. Bringing Candy to the bed, he helped her kneel on it, then took position behind her on his own haunches. Candy's heart began to race, wondering what new trick Dev was up to.

"We need something special for this time," Dev purred in her ear. "Raise your hands above your head."

Candy raised them, then felt the fur-lined cuffs as they snapped to her wrists, keeping her arms above her. Dev's hands traveled down from her secured hands, whispered across her soft shoulder skin, then slipped down her chest to cup her breasts.

"Tell me you want me," Dev whispered, kissing her throat as his fingers massaged her already swelling teats. He moved slightly, rubbing his engorged penis in the cleft of Candy's buttocks.

"I want you," Candy whispered.

Dev reached down, his hand touching her soft pubic hair, then rubbing gently. At once, Candy's labia moistened in response, the circular motion stirring her lust as her body readied her for penetration. But Dev just continued to stroke, unhurried. The fires in Candy's loins grew until an inferno raged, and her juices coated his dexterous fingers.

Just when she thought she would have to beg him, Dev kissed her throat, then whispered "up on your knees."

Candy complied, shivering in anticipation when she felt the slick press of Devlin's smooth head rub against her wet folds, then slide partway inside. She wanted more than anything to push back, to bury that long, wonderful throbbing length deep inside her. But she remembered Vicky, and waited.

"Good girl," Dev breathed in her ear. "Just stay still for me."

Devlin pressed himself, the head of his cock entering, then withdrawing. On the next thrust, just a little more entered, the shaft sliding in before withdrawing. Again and again, Dev pushed inside, until at last he was buried in her, filling her completely. With a groan, Dev's head went back, and then he began to move in earnest, clutching her hips as he rammed into her.

"God you feel good," he groaned. "I can't wait, Candy..."

One hand buried itself in her pubic hair, even as Dev's other held her hip stationary. The moment he touched her swollen clit, Candy felt the stirrings of orgasm. With each successive rub and thrust, another notch was raised and the feeling built, the languid joy that it could not be stopped making her head loll in her bondage.

Dev's thrusting grew deeper, his movements longer, as he moved his organ to stroke Candy, even as his hand possessed her, the spiraling bliss making her pant as she fought to keep still. Then with a burst of feeling she reached the peak and fell, screaming in pleasure, her back arching as she fought to wring every last spasm from her orgasm.

Candy sagged back against Dev, and he wrapped his arms around her. He held her as she quieted, then slid back into her and began moving. Candy was so surprised that she turned to look at him.

"You were denied too often in your life," Dev said, his eyes glowing with lust. "This is my gift to you, my bloodlover."

"I can't...I can't do it again," Candy said raggedly. "I can still feel the aftershocks of the first—"

"Let yourself ride them to another," Dev said, his hand again busy in her snatch. He thrust slowly in and out, again rubbing her all over inside.

Amazingly, Candy felt the stirrings of another orgasm again, faintly. She closed her eyes, willing the sensations to rise, concentrating on the feeling of Dev's manipulation.

This time the orgasm seemed to come almost immediately. Candy cried out, bliss filling her as she rode the waves again to fruition.

Again, Dev held her as she sagged, and again, when she had quieted, he began again. This time, the stirrings were fainter, more elusive, the orgasm like a fleeing rabbit that she had to catch. But with concentration and Devlin's ministrations, she was soon gasping out her release again. As she came, Dev spanked her three times hard, then came himself, shuddering as he yelled. This time, Dev uncuffed her hands, then helped her lay down, covering them both with a comforter.

"Holy shit," Candy said raggedly. "I can't believe it."

"Multiple orgasms are usually possible for women," Dev said, kissing her cheek. "Men are too eager to come themselves, oafs that they are."

"Could I have come again?" Candy asked, eager.

"In time, most likely," Devlin said, nodding. "But you felt that the second and third were weaker, yes?"

Candy nodded.

"Know when to stop in that regard, also," Devlin said. "Or you will give yourself a headache trying too hard."

Candy tittered with laughter, then hugged him. "Thank you."

"Thank you," Dev said seductively, pulling her close.

An hour before dawn, Dev rose, and began dressing. Candy watched him from the bed, worried and also in awe.

"You watch me as if you're not sure you'll ever see me again." Dev turned to her, fully dressed. "Why, when I told you I will see you?"

"Because I'm worried about you walking out that door and never feeling again what I felt tonight with you."

Dev smiled. "Are we having a Dirty Dancing moment?"

Candy tried to smile, and couldn't, she was too upset. "I can't go back to just pretending, now that I know what coming feels like. I want more."

Dev came and sat beside her. "You can orgasm with any man, Candy. It was only your belief that you couldn't come that had stopped you." He kissed her hand. "And I will see you again, I promise." He reached into his pocket, withdrew his wallet, and handed her a card. "Call me to make arrangements."

Candy read the card. "Devlin Dalcon. I like the sound of that. French?"

"Yes," Dev said, pleased.

"How would Friday of next week be?" Candy offered.

"I'll send a car for you," Devlin replied, standing. He kissed her hand, flashed her a last slow smile, then sauntered out the bedroom door.

THE END

THE NEWLYWEDS

NANCY PIRRI

Jane laughed off her new husband's threats to turn her over his knee if she disobeyed him, but soon realizes he's serious on their honeymoon. Humiliated and furious, she threatens him with divorce but Aaron convinces her to give them a chance. Jane soon realizes Aaron is exactly the kind of man she needs in her life.

1

J ane Cassidy cringed as she thought about her little accident today when she had left home for the courthouse. As she sat in the Ramsey County Courthouse Cafeteria eating lunch, she thought about the pathetic condition of her brand new car.

Five hours ago, she'd sat behind the wheel of her new Mini Cooper, afraid to look in her rearview mirror. When she finally did, she saw that one side of the white picket fence that surrounded her yard was tilting over. Putting the car in park she opened the door, jumped out and strode to the back of the car, groaning in dismay at her crunched back left fender.

Aaron will be furious!

Hadn't he told her not to drive the new car until he had time to take her out for some driving lessons? She'd recently gotten her driver's license back, after it had been suspended for several months due to too many speeding and traffic violations. She hated to admit it but faced the truth of the matter; she was a horrid driver and needed more practice.

Her husband hadn't figured out how she'd passed the driving test in the first place. Jane hadn't felt the need to tell him she'd merely charmed the pants off the driving examiner, convincing him to pass her. She couldn't help but blame her parents for her awful driving since they hadn't allowed her to get her driver's license until after she'd turned eighteen. Admittedly, she'd been a wild girl—an only child of elderly parents—and denying her a driver's license had seemed to be the only way they could control her behavior. Now she was twenty-four years old and her driving hadn't improved much over the past four years.

Aaron had said she needed a lot more practice before she could drive alone. Since totaling her car during their engagement, it had taken her nearly a year to save enough money for a down payment on the Mini Cooper she'd purchased. She'd had the car already a month and her busy attorney husband never seemed to have the time to give her those promised driving lessons.

This morning, she'd awakened late for work. If Aaron had been home he would have roused her from her slumber so she wouldn't be late, then would have driven her to work with him since they both worked downtown at the Ramsey County Courthouse—he as a prosecuting attorney—her as a court reporter. But she'd overslept, mostly because she'd tossed and turned all night long due to Aaron being gone on an overnight trip for his job. She wasn't used to sleeping alone and had missed him during the long night hours.

Not wanting to be late, she'd grabbed the keys for the new car this morning—then promptly backed into her own fence.

Jane could just hear him scolding now; *didn't I warn you not to drive until I'd given you driving lessons?* Then he'd turn her over his knee and spank her bottom until it was rosy, hot, and stinging, and tears were streaming down her cheeks.

Aaron had set the ground rules shortly after he proposed to her, saying he took to heart their wedding vows—his promise to love and protect—hers to love, honor and obey. She'd thought it sweet at the time and hadn't taken him seriously, until she'd disobeyed him.

Jane shuddered, remembering the one time he'd punished her, she knew he'd meant every word; knew for certain that he was an old-fashioned man with old-fashioned ideas where his wife was concerned. She also knew he was overly-protective of her, and driving the when she wasn't competent (in his mind) would drive him over the edge.

Jane had learned that painful lesson while on their honeymoon, near the end of a glorious Mexican vacation. Aaron had many connections in his work as a prosecuting attorney, and had subleased a house on a private length of beach for them. On the last day of their honeymoon, he'd told her not to go swimming, due to the recent warning about shark-infested waters near their beachfront. But Jane wasn't going to let any shark threat keep her away from the balmy aqua blue water in which she loved to swim, thinking it could be years before they had the chance at another vacation like this.

Also, his verbal threat to paddle her bottom had made her laugh. She'd told him, "This isn't the eighteenth century but the twenty-first. Men don't spank their wives. And if they did they'd be hauled off to jail for wife abuse." He'd simply shrugged his shoulders and said he'd given her clear, fair warning and would follow through with his threats if she disobeyed him. He could care less whether she called the cops on him or not.

Her first mistake—she believed he was bluffing. Her second—disobeying him. On that fateful day, while he'd been showering, she'd gone swimming anyway. When she rose from the water after swimming for several minutes and headed for the beach, she looked up and saw Aaron standing near her beach towel, which had fallen from a sturdy chair beside a picnic table with an umbrella in the center. He wore his swimming trunks, displaying his long, tanned, muscular legs and broad chest, and she was glad he decided to join her.

His windswept hair, slightly long and golden, was a brilliant contrast next to her chin-length inky tresses. They also contrasted in their body builds as well. Where he was tall and muscular, she was petite, but full of womanly curves, as her husband would say, in all the right places. She loved his body as he loved hers. Then she'd seen the look in his eyes and knew he'd meant every warning he'd given her. Her body started trembling, thinking how she'd never seen such a harsh look on his face in the year and half they'd known each other.

Slowly, she made her way to where he stood. Stopping before him she tilted up her chin, gave him a cool, long look.

"Damn it, woman, have you a hearing problem?" he snapped.

"I hear just fine," she said. "You are my husband, not my lord and master. As you can see no shark dared take a bite out of me."

"You heard the shark reports today. Why would you purposely go swimming when I told you not to? Do you have a death wish or something? Or, are you looking to just rile me?"

She sighed. "I stood by the water's edge and saw no fins sticking out of the water. I figured this could be the last time in a while that I take a nice vacation anywhere knowing how busy your work schedule is."

"This could have been the *last* vacation you ever took!"

"Lighten up, honey," she said, giving him one of her usually irresistible, sexy smiles. "You're making a big deal out of nothing." She saw his eyes flare with even more fury, but she chose to ignore him, which was a huge mistake.

Jane bent down to pick up her towel from the sand, but was unable to rise from her bent over position. Aaron kept her down, his hand pressing on the nape of her neck.

"Uh, Aaron? What are you doing?" She shivered, recalling his threat, her heart hammering at the thought that he possibly meant to carry it out. Her body, clad in a tiny shocking pink bikini bottom and top, offered little protection.

Instinctively, she pulled her arms behind her to cover her ass but it did no good for he brushed them aside. "I warned you." His softly spoken words were quickly followed by the smack of his big hand against one ass cheek.

She yelped in surprise and flailed her arms against his hold, to no avail.

"Your ass is going to be pink as the suit you're wearing when I'm through with you. My order today, to stay out of the water, was simply that, an order, not a suggestion. When I give an order, I mean for it to be followed."

"Like hell..." she began, gasping with surprise when he started spanking her in earnest, punishing first one cheek, then the other. She squirmed beneath his tight grip on her neck but couldn't escape his hold. By the twentieth smack, (she'd counted!) she remembered how her initial, indignant shrieks had been replaced by painful, contrite sobs. Each spank came a bit harder and he showed no signs of letting up.

Jane tried a different tactic—kicking back her feet, catching him in the calf.

"Oh, no, you don't. You're not going anywhere yet," he said as he wound his left arm over her back and under her stomach. Then he planted the sole of one bare foot on the chair's seat, lifting her so she dangled over his thigh, feet off the sand. He shifted her body forward over his knee so that she had to plant her hands on the chair's seat edge to keep her balance, but the position also left her ass raised high to the heavens and vulnerable.

Beneath the shade of the umbrella, he continued where he'd left off. The only thing she was thankful for was that he hadn't taken down her bikini bottom, though it afforded little protection, and they had their own private beach and no one had seen her humiliation.

Her sobs didn't make any difference to him for his punishing palm continued to blaze a wicked heat over her ass. She could barely reply to his blaring reprimands but eventually managed to say, "Yes, you told me! I should have listened to you! Please stop!"

He didn't stop but said, "Sorry, you're not getting off that easily, Jane. Your punishment is far from over."

He kept pelting her ass in an even cadence. She hung over his knee, unable to do anything but sob her heart out. She learned something else that day; the more she struggled against him the more punishment she received, which was food for thought for the future—that is if they even had one anymore! When he finally released her, she stood on trembling legs, unable to believe he'd treated her so horribly.

Her tears and sadness subsided, followed by an anger she'd never felt before toward anyone in her life. She swung her hand and slapped him across one cheek. "How dare you!" she exploded before stalking off to their beach house and locking herself in the bathroom. Luckily, she'd left her cell phone in the bathroom that morning for once she stopped crying she called the police and reported her husband's abuse. Soon one lone Mexican policeman arrived on their doorstep.

Jane sat on the sofa clad in her bikini still but had tossed on a long sleeved white shirt to cover up her body. Scowling, she listened to the conversation between her groom and the cop, unable to understand a word of the Spanish they spoke. She'd had no idea her husband knew fluent Spanish and, unfortunately, she knew not a single word. But when the cop sent a chiding look at her, then grinned at her husband and smacked him on the back, she knew she would get no help from that arena.

2

After the cop left, her husband spared her a brief scowl, went to his briefcase, and took out an old-fashioned wooden ruler. Her eyes widened on the ruler and she rose from the sofa when he headed toward her, an implacable expression on his face. Without a word, he caught her behind the couch, pressed her forward over the back of it. She saw his arm go up and started protesting, "No, damn you! Not again."

"Yes, again, and again, until you learn when I tell you 'no', I mean it," he said between gritted teeth. "Didn't I tell you calling the police would do you no good? That cop was on my side and completely understood what a brat you were to disobey an order meant to protect you."

Jane looked over her shoulder and saw his mouth thinned in concentration, his gaze focused on her ass as he raised his arm. Then she saw it come down and she howled in pain and outrage when the first spank hit one already abused cheek. Catching her breath after the next spank, she howled through the next dozen smacks, her ass feeling hot and raw, until he finally stopped and moved away from her, returning the ruler to his briefcase.

Between her tears, she saw the disgust on his face. Turning away, she collapsed on the seat of the sofa and buried her head in her arms over the couch's arm. She was hurt, humiliated, and angry at the injustice and brutish behavior from her husband—a man she'd been madly in love with—a man she believed had been madly in love with her.

After a while, she looked up and saw him nowhere in sight. She stumbled out to the deck to find him sitting in a chair, staring out at the ocean.

"As soon as we get home I'm filing for divorce," she announced.

His head whipped around and she almost caved at his pained expression, but the overwhelming pain in her bottom, which she now rubbed carefully, stopped her. If he'd apologized then and there, and promised to never treat her like a child again, she might have reconsidered, but he didn't. Instead, he said, "If you think, based on what's happened here, that a judge will issue a divorce because of this one incident then you're dead wrong. No divorce, Jane."

"Minnesota is no fault divorce, darling," she said sweetly. "And I don't need much reason to divorce you and you know it."

"In the year and a half we've known each other I never realized you were such a brat, and so unreasonable," he growled, rising to his feet. He stood before her, towering over her five-two stature. Jamming his hands on his hips he snarled, "Since I'm an attorney I know the ropes and I won't make it easy on you."

Tears filled her eyes and her voice trembled with her reply, "You are so nasty. How could you have fooled me so?"

"I warned you before we married that I'm an old-fashioned guy, remember?"

"I thought you were joking! You're nothing like the man I thought you were. You're nothing but a brute!"

He shrugged. "Now you know I wasn't joking."

She recalled him telling her so in conversation that he had to be the dominant partner in their marriage. They'd been dating for several months and had been sleeping together, their relationship back then based on pure, unmitigated lust. She'd heard him but hadn't thought much about his casual comments at the time. He'd always been kind, sweet and gentle to her, though she recalled his playful side when he'd give her love taps on the buttocks. Those she hadn't minded at all! She'd fallen madly in love with him over the several months they dated.

His face softened. Reaching out, he took her arms and drew her close. "All that I did today was because I love you, remember that."

She scoffed and pulled out of his arms. "You've an awful way of showing your love. I don't believe you."

"When I came out of the bathroom and saw you'd left the condominium, I had no idea where you'd gone. When I saw you down by the beach, in the water, I was worried sick about you. If you don't think that's love, then I don't know what is," he finished before entering the beach house and slamming the front door on his way out of the house.

Their airplane trip home the next day had been accomplished in an uncomfortable silence. When Jane entered their home, she burst into sobs as she stared at the presents from their wedding in the spare bedroom they hadn't even unwrapped yet. He'd left the house immediately after dropping off his luggage, without uttering a word as to where he was going.

That evening, after Jane had unpacked, she had second thoughts about leaving him. She loved him still, though she'd never forgive him for taking her over his knee. But was a spanking enough of a reason to leave him? It wasn't as though he'd beat her up—it was discipline, pure and simple—on her well-cushioned buttocks.

Her conscience niggled at her too, then, as she thought about his worrying over her swimming. She'd always been a rather spoiled only child and had rarely listened to her parents' orders. By the time she was fourteen she lived her life the way she wanted, having had several minor brushes with the law. But, simply put, her parents could not control her and, though they'd threatened her plenty, they'd never followed through with their threats of discipline—with the one exception—their refusal to allow her to drive.

Consequently, she'd been an independent soul for several years, used to doing what she wanted to do, when and how. Now she was blessed with a husband who expected her to buckle under his authority. *Why can't I?* she asked herself, especially when she knew Aaron to be a rational man—a caring man—a just man. He was a high-powered prosecuting attorney who always thought logically. She prayed he'd return tonight so they could sit down and have a rational discussion since she didn't really want a divorce.

Luckily, she had food in the house and she quickly made sautéed chicken breasts in olive oil and seasonings with wild rice and frozen asparagus. Not a feast but good enough she hoped she could convince him to stay, eat, and talk. Quickly, she changed into a clean pair of warm moleskin pink slacks and pink angora sweater that she knew Aaron loved.

Just when she'd turned off the oven, Aaron came in, looking exhausted and wary. She invited him to eat dinner.

"Why?" he asked, as he pulled off his winter coat, "So you can poison me?"

Her feelings had been hurt at his words but she said softly, "I've had time to think over what happened between us and am having second thoughts about a divorce."

She saw the relieved look on his face as he expelled his breath and sat down at the dining room table with her. They ate in silence, their eyes flitting to each other then away through the meal. When they finished eating Jane opened up the conversation.

"Like I said, I've had time to reconsider and don't want a divorce."

He gave her a small smile. "But can you live with a brutish man, as you called me? Can you live your life with a man who has no qualms about punishing you for misbehaving?"

She almost pouted, defensive at his words, but changed her mind. "Can you give me instances of what you're talking about?"

"When I say 'no' to you about something that concerns your safety, or making important decisions in our marriage, do you understand I'm the final authority and will always have the final say?"

"All right. I'll concede that the safety issue at the beach you were justified in reprimanding me, but what about you?"

"What about me?"

"Do I have the right to do the same to you?"

He raised his brow. "What? You mean spank me if I misbehave?"

She started laughing and, after taking a small sip of her wine, said, "It sounds silly, doesn't it?"

He nodded. "It does. Besides, and I know you won't like to hear this, but it goes back to what I told you earlier, about my being an old-fashioned guy. A man has the authority in a marriage, in his family, not the woman. I truly believe that."

She frowned. "Why hadn't you told me this during the eighteen months we dated before marrying?"

"I enjoyed our easy conversation, the way we were with each other. We had so many common interests, and you are an unbelievably gifted, social person. I grew to love you and, frankly, learned to appreciate your independent streak, but then you always behaved responsibly. I figured as long as you made good decisions I didn't have to broach my views on a husband being the dominant partner and the wife being submissive."

Jane cringed. "God, I hate that word."

He smiled. "Submissive?" At her nod, he laughed. "Being submissive has its rewards, honey, believe me. Every woman I've dated, until you, has allowed me to be the dominant partner."

"So why did you marry me then if you knew I wasn't... submissive," she spat.

Frowning, he said, "I guess I figured you to be mature and as rational as me, not to mention the fact you're every bit as smart. Since you seemed so mature, I figured when we eventually disagreed about something you'd see things my way. Obviously, this didn't prove to be the case."

"I have to admit," Jane said, "that your order to stay out of the water prompted me to want to do the exact opposite. I didn't like your tone. It reminded me of how my father used to talk to me."

He frowned. "I have no desire to be paternal toward you, Jane. Did your father beat you? If so, I guess I can understand your hesitancy to be married to a dominant man."

Jane shook her head and laughed. "Hell, no. My father never beat me... in hindsight, he probably should have. I've told you about my wild days of youth and run ins with the law. Neither my father nor mother could handle me. I suppose in a way, I've still got a bit of the wild child in me."

"Yes, I've learned that during the past week," he replied.

"So, where do your old-fashioned guy theories come from?"

"My father. Believe me, I spent plenty of time over his knee," he laughed.

"What about your mother?"

With a groan, Aaron said, "I've never been privy to that information, and don't ever want to be. But I imagine my mother was... well... rather rebellious at one time. How my father handled her I can't imagine."

Jane thought about Aaron Cassidy, Senior, Aaron's distinguished father who had also been a powerhouse attorney before retiring a few years ago. Then she thought about his vivacious, beautiful mother and tried imagining her over her husband's knee for misbehaving. Surprisingly, as she thought about it, she could very well imagine Claire Cassidy being disciplined. She was an outgoing, outspoken woman. Jane could easily imagine her butting heads with her husband.

"How long have your parents been married?"

"Thirty-seven years."

"Wow. That's a life-time, isn't it?" Raising her gaze to meet his humor-filled one she added, "How did your mother tolerate that… that sort of treatment from your father all those years?"

Aaron threw back his head and laughed. "As I said, I have no idea how father handled my mother, but if he did, she likely learned, as I did, that once the rules were set she had no choice. Actually, they got along famously."

"You mean once he took your mother to task as you did me?"

He shrugged. "Perhaps, though my parents never came right out and talked about this, it was something I suspected." Leaning across the table, he took her hand and said softly, "So, think you can you live with an overbearing brute like me or not?"

Hesitantly, she said, "I'll try." Frowning, she added, "But I don't ever want to feel I'm walking on eggshells around you, Aaron. It's not right. It makes me feel inferior to you."

He released her hand, came around the table, and pulled her up to stand in front of him. Winding an arm around her waist he settled her against his chest, dipped his mouth down to hers. Jane stopped breathing at the exquisite sensation of his lips caressing hers.

"Let's keep things simple then to begin with. I certainly don't want you feeling apprehensive and scared around me, darling. Safety issues to begin with and financial decisions in our marriage fall on my shoulders. Is that too much to ask?"

"Financial issues? You don't expect me to give up my own checking and savings accounts do you?"

"Absolutely not. You work hard for your money. Keep your money. I'm talking about when we make decisions on big purchases, that sort of thing, that I have the final say."

Before she could reply, he settled his lips on hers again, slanting them, licking them until she gasped in delight. Then, when his hand slid from her waist and down between them, settling on her naked thigh she relaxed against him. He held her up with one arm around her waist, the other unbuttoning her slacks. They slid down her legs and he lifted her away from them. Then he dispensed with her thong and settled her on a long section of kitchen countertop. Aaron spread her thighs apart, unsnapped his jeans, and dropped them, moving between her thighs.

"Agreed?" he murmured against her lips.

Foggy now, trying to remember their earlier conversation, and wanting all talk to end and feelings to begin, Jane replied, "Yes. Now make love to me," she ordered.

His lips slid down her neck, to her breast. He sucked the nipple between his lips, which caused shivers down her spine. She arched her back, welcoming his touch.

3

Now, on this cold February day, Jane sat in the cafeteria, having lost all track of time. She smiled when she thought about how he'd made love to her that day six months ago. How they made love often still, and how she had learned to crave his touch.

Since their honeymoon, he'd not been the brutish, controlling, dominant husband, but treated her as an equal. But then, he'd had no cause to treat her any differently since she hadn't disobeyed those two rules he'd set; her safety and financial issues, which made her think, would her smashing her new Mini into their front yard fence be considered a safety issue? Most likely not, but then she thought about the outcome if she had managed to drive away in it, without the required lessons from her husband.

She groaned and dropped her head onto her folded arms on the table.

Aaron was seven years older than her twenty-four years. She hadn't really thought the age gap all that significant, until now, when she thought about him taking her over his knee and spanking her in a very paternal manner, as though she were a naughty little girl, even though he'd said he had no desire to be a paternal figure in her life. She couldn't help feeling that way, though.

She rose from her seat and headed to the courtroom to report her next scheduled case, coming to a decision. She would accept his discipline because she'd made a mistake. She knew she had it coming, and would cooperate fully. And she'd still love him when the session was over.

She arrived at work early the next day, reported during two trials before breaking for lunch in the courthouse cafeteria. There she met up with Clarice Johnson, another court reporter and close friend from high school.

"You done for the day?" Clarice asked her.

"One more and I will be. How about you?"

"I'm finished and meeting my husband for dinner tonight at The Buttery. Can you get a hold of Aaron and see if you two can join us?"

Jane shook her head. "He's out of town until the weekend."

"Oh, well, next time."

Clarice started to rise when Jane said, "Could I talk to you about something?"

"Of course." Clarice sat, sinking down at the table again. "Checking her watch, she said, "I've got an extra ten minutes." When Jane didn't start, Clarice said, "Go ahead. I'm listening."

Jane smiled and felt her cheeks heat up. "I'm not sure where to begin."

"How about from the beginning? That's always a good place."

Jane did, and told Clarice about what had happened on her honeymoon and more recently about the car.

"Whew," Clarice said, sinking back in her chair. "He's going to be really mad, isn't he?"

Jane nodded.

"Can you blame him?"

Frowning Jane said, "Are you taking his side on this?"

"Whoa! Wait a minute. I'm not taking sides at all. I'm making an observation here. Don't you think he has a right to be angry with you, though?"

"I know he does. But do you think its right he treats me like a child over something like this?"

Clarice stunned her when she said, "Sure do."

"What!"

"How can you argue you did nothing wrong and don't need punishment when you do?" Clarice countered. She sat forward and added, "Look, Harry and I have I guess what you'd call a traditional marriage, too."

Jane's eyes widened. "You've got to be kidding?"

Clarice laughed. "What? You think because I'm two inches taller and twenty-five pounds heavier than my Harry that he can't whoop my ass for being a brat?"

"No! That's not what I thought at all. It's just that this is the twenty-first century, not the dark ages. Why would a woman want a man to treat her that way?"

"I can't tell you about other women but will tell you why I do. I've never been a feminine woman, you know? I mean, I'm this tall German built on the bigger girl size. But believe me, there's nothing that makes me feel more cherished and feminine than having my Harry be the boss."

Jane gave a covert look around her. "So, you're serious. He has... well, I think you get my drift."

"Yes, he has spanked me," Clarice said with a laugh. "When I've deserved it, which hasn't been too often, but often enough I remember the pain of it, feel the remorse for my actions, and then love my Harry even more for caring." Now Clarice was the one looking around and speaking softly, "We also indulge ourselves in 'play spanking sessions' too and have the best sex afterwards you can imagine."

"What!"

"You heard me," Clarice said, chuckling. "There's just some mental exchange of unbelievable happiness that happens between us after a session. Oh, I don't at all enjoy the disciplinary spankings but the other? Holy cow, they're fantastic. Harry makes me feel like a woman—the only woman he'll ever need."

Jane smiled. "You really love him and it sounds like you've found what works for you in your marriage."

"We have. I feel lucky and blessed. You can have that, too. Have you ever had a 'play session' with Aaron before?"

"No! I can't imagine having a session over his knee for fun and to achieve sexual satisfaction."

She shrugged. "Try it sometime. You may change your mind."

Over the next two days, Jane gave some consideration to Clarice's suggestion. But then she wondered how she would ever be brave enough to even ask Aaron for that kind of 'kink' in their bed. But then she thought about how he enjoyed taking her from behind, doggy-style he'd called it. She also remembered how, a few times he'd ridden her from behind and alternated reaming her vagina ruthlessly, while smacking her thighs. She couldn't deny those slaps excited her, and drove her on to achieving some of the most explosive orgasms she'd ever had, so perhaps she would enjoy playful spankings, though she knew she hated the disciplinary ones.

They hadn't voiced their sexual preferences to each other but, through Aaron's lead in bed she'd followed in most of his desires, with the exception of anal sex. It didn't sound at all appealing to her.

Now she tried to think of a way to broach the 'play sessions', as Clarice called them, to Aaron, her body tingling at the thought. Somehow, she didn't think Aaron would go for such an idea. He seemed to equate discipline with her misbehavior and not with having sexual fun still, she'd find a way to broach the subject to him—at the right time.

Aaron arrived home late Friday evening, therefore it was dark and he didn't see the dent in her Mini Cooper or the leaning fence. And he parked in the second garage located in back of their house. Jane was already in bed, though she was awake. Thankfully, neither of them had work Saturday morning so they could make love tonight—as often as they wanted—then 'sleep in' in the morning. Jane knew she'd get her comeuppance then and she cringed at the thought, but she did have it coming to her.

"Darling? You awake?" he asked when he entered their bedroom.

Jane rolled over and turned on the small bedside light. "Uh-huh." She smiled at him and lifted her arms to him. "Yes, and waiting for you."

They made love that night twice before falling asleep.

Jane was rudely awakened the following morning to the sound of Aaron's cursing and slamming their bedroom door. She sat up in bed, brushing her bangs back from her forehead to find Aaron standing shirtless in the doorway, jeans on but unsnapped. She sighed, loving the view, enjoyed how the light sprinkling of golden hair arrowed down below his beltline and over his abdomen. Lifting her gaze, she met his eyes and her body went cold at the anger simmering in them.

"Come outside. Now," he said.

Damn! He'd discovered the car. After scrambling from bed, she tugged on her jeans and old University of Minnesota sweatshirt. Snatching her fleece jacket from the closet, she pulled it on and headed out the door. She found Aaron standing near the damaged fender on the Mini Cooper, still shirtless, even though it was below freezing and a blanket of snow covered the ground.

Pausing beside him, he pointed at the fender. "Know anything about this?"

After hitting the fence three days ago, she hadn't moved the car back inside the garage, as she should have. She didn't want to move the car, for fear of bumping into the garage when driving it back inside.

She nodded, gave him a pitiful look. "I did it. I'm sorry. I was late for work on Tuesday, and—"

"You mean you took the Mini out of the garage to drive it downtown to work?" At her nod he scolded, "Didn't I tell you that you couldn't drive the new car until I'd given you several driving lessons?"

"You did, but darn it, Aaron, you're never around to give me a lesson!" she exploded. "We've had the car over a month and it's been sitting in the garage all this time."

His dour expression seemed to soften and he sighed. "You're right. I thought I'd have time to teach you last week but got called out of town. Sorry about that. Still, that doesn't excuse the fact you tried taking the car when I expressly told you not to."

"I paid for this car, you know. I should be able to take it anytime I want."

"True, but not until after you've had some much needed driving lessons first." As though he suddenly realized he was standing outside in the cold without a shirt, he wound his arms around himself. "Let's go inside and talk."

She followed him into the house, encouraged by his comment. Talk, he'd said, not spank.

In the house, he pointed at the couch. "Sit. I'll get us coffee."

Relieved for the reprieve, she was encouraged he was willing to talk. She was beginning to think, hopefully, that the wrecked fender and taking the car without his permission didn't fall, by his rules, within the safety and financial areas so she breathed a relieved sigh and leaned back against the couch. He returned with two cups of coffee, passed one to her and sat down beside her.

After they took a few sips, he set his cup down and turned to her, his arm sliding across the back of the sofa as he faced her. "I know you didn't mean to damage the car, sweetheart, but you did. Luckily you didn't take it out on the street, which would have been hazardous to your health, knowing how little you drive, and your lack of competency."

She bristled and set her cup down. "You know, Aaron, I drove myself around for several years before I met you."

"And how many tickets and accidents have you had during those years?"

"That's beside the point."

"No, it's not," he said firmly. "It's only recently you finally paid off all the fines for the tickets that had been issued, not to mention the last speeding ticket you received was only eight months ago."

"Before we were married."

"Doesn't matter. I paid a lot of money out of my pocket to help you pay those fines. Which gets me to the next point. You've punishment coming you know. I hate to do it, but—"

"Hold on! How does my damaging the fender harm my safety or cause us any financial grief when I didn't get out of the driveway and insurance will pay to replace the fender?"

"There was potential for you to get hurt driving the car. Our insurance premium could go up because you caused the accident, and no other car was involved."

She saw his point but said, voice wheedling, "Can't we wait to hear back on the damages from the insurance company first?"

He shook his head, shoved the coffee table into the center of the room, then took her hands in his. "It's bad enough you could have been hurt when I was away. How do you think I would have felt about that if you'd had an accident on the way to work? So, I'm adding one more area that deserves punishment; when I tell you 'no' to *anything*, that means 'no'. Come on now," he said calmly, her wrists in his big hands and pulling her toward him, "Let's get this over with."

4

J ane just couldn't cooperate because she didn't agree with his rationale. She pulled her hands out of his grasp and jumped to her feet. "No, darn it, Aaron, you can't just change the rules because you want to! There will be plenty of times I say 'no' to you about things and you'll say 'no' to me. This, in my opinion, doesn't warrant punishment. You're just trying to find an excuse to spank me, that's all."

He frowned and folded his arms as he stared up at her. "Now, why in the hell would I do that? Do you think I enjoy spanking you?"

"In a way, yes, I do."

"How?" he asked softly.

"I just think you do, that's all. Some people do enjoy that sort of, well, you know what I mean."

"Love play?"

"Guess you could call it that, though you blistering my ass isn't a bit playful or loving."

His smile widened. "With whom have you been discussing our marriage?"

She gulped. "Nobody."

"Don't add lying to your offenses."

She gulped again. "All right. I had a discussion with my friend, Clarice."

"Ah," he said.

"Ah? What in the hell does that mean?"

"I think I know where you're going with this discussion, that's all it means."

"And how would you know?"

"Because Clarice's husband, Harry, belongs to the same men's club I belong to. I know him well."

"You do?" Jane asked in surprise. At his nod she asked, narrowing her eyes, "And just what all happens at this men's club? You always evaded me when I asked in the past."

"It doesn't matter since I don't go there much any longer."

"It matters."

"All right. It's men only, of course, and besides all of the exercise equipment and swimming pool we use, we hold manly discussions on how to handle our women."

"You what!"

He laughed. "Very informal, over a cocktail, that's all."

"How much is discussed?"

"You asking how in-depth the men talk about their women?" He shrugged. "It varies, depending on the man. Harry, for instance, was very talkative. I still find it hard to imagine Harry taking the tall, voluptuous Clarice over his lap and paddling her bottom, but he claimed he does. What did Clarice say?"

"She said as much, and I find it hard to believe, too." Haltingly, she added, "She also mentioned they enjoy the love play sessions, which sound very nice. Couldn't we do that instead of you punishing me?"

Softly, as he rose to his feet, he said, "Love play sessions are sexual. My punishing you for wrong-doing is not—it's discipline, pure and simple. There is a difference. One is meant to be pleasurable while the other, painful."

"I know, but, when you aren't disciplining me... I'm just curious about trying it."

He took her in his arms, kissed her full on the lips. She sighed, wound her arms around his neck, giving herself up to him and his enticing kiss. Breaking away, he replied, "I have been trying to figure out a way to broach that particular subject with you since before we married."

Her eyes widened. "Well, why didn't you come right out and ask then?"

Ducking his forehead against hers, he murmured, "I didn't want to scare you off and think I was some pervert or woman-beater."

"You are neither. You are a fair, wonderful husband. I'm a lucky girl."

"Even if, in a moment, you'll be on the receiving end of my punishment?"

She sniffed, "Even then."

"Go to our room and prepare yourself."

She looked at him, confused. "I don't know what you mean."

From now on, when I deal out a punishment spanking you will remove all your clothes and position yourself over the end of our bed."

Jane's eyes widened. "Must I?"

"Yes. Normally, a punishment spanking is impersonally delivered."

"Wouldn't you say removing my clothes is rather personal?"

He grinned. "True, but it also contributes to a sense of humiliation, too, being completely defenseless and unclothed."

She nodded. "As you said earlier, let's get this over with."

A aron went to the garage to retrieve his old fraternity paddle, one he'd fashioned himself as a freshman in college. It was made of oak, sixteen inches long, half an inch thick and drilled with several holes. He'd forgotten about it until today, recalling he'd seen it tucked away in a box on the top shelf when looking for other things a few weeks ago. Needless to say, he'd had a few first hand experiences being on the receiving end of the paddle in his fraternity, knowing well it packed a memorable wallop.

He wasn't looking forward to disciplining his wife the second time in six months, but he'd set the terms of their marriage and she would abide by them. He knew she was remorseful already, but she wouldn't get out of this necessary punishment, and he wouldn't go easy on her. She deserved it. She could have driven off, had an accident, and harmed herself.

He thought about her lying in the hospital with injuries or worse, dead, and he hardened his heart. Already, knowing how he hated hurting her, he'd decided to make this session a short but painful one so that it wouldn't need to be repeated for a long, long time.

Walking into their bedroom, he was pleased to find her draped over the end of the bed, her legs hanging down, thighs closed tight together, which he decided needed readjusting. She was too short for her feet to touch the floor, though, which meant he'd have a hell of a time containing her flailing legs. Her arms were folded with her head resting on them. She had her eyes closed, her head turned away from him. She was unaware of his presence.

With no warning, he moved up behind her, recalled how he'd been swatted in the fraternity the first time with an over-handed then under-handed smack, wincing even now at the memory of the excruciating pain. As part of his initiation, he'd endured that double-whammy brutal swat from every upperclassman in the fraternity, a total of forty hits. He hadn't been able to sit comfortably for a week.

He worried then about Jane and decided he'd wield the paddle with a lighter hand.

Drawing his hand back and over his head, he brought it down with what he believed was a light stroke, smacking the upper area of one pleasingly plump ass cheek—followed up with a second, an under-handed one on the same cheek.

Jane had started wailing with the first slap, escalating into a loud shriek with the second. "Aw, Aaron!" she shouted, scrambling to her feet and dancing before him in a frantic haphazard fashion, her hands covering her buttocks.

He had to admit she made a fetching picture performing her painful dance, stark naked with her hands covering her ass, a scowl on her face, her bountiful breasts bobbing up and down.

Returning to business, he said, "We'll try a different position. This one is too low."

"Are you trying to kill me with that thing? Where did it come from?" She glared in horror at the paddle.

"It's my old college frat paddle. All the guys made one as part of the initiation process. And believe me I know what it feels like."

"My God, I thought hazing was outlawed years ago!"

"Political correctness is rampant in colleges, true, but there are frat societies that conceal this aspect of initiation into the membership. Frat paddling still exists, according to my nephew, a freshman in college who just underwent the ritual."

"Why can't you just use your hand?"

He frowned. "My hand won't be as effective. Besides, if I use the paddle you'll receive less spanks and your punishment will be done sooner."

"Oh. Well, I guess that's okay, but why shorten it?"

He raised his brow. "Like I said, I've been on the receiving end of this thing. Believe me, a few smacks is equivalent to ten hand delivered ones."

She bit her lip worriedly. "I don't think I want you to use it on me."

He watched the horror spreading on her face, clutching her ass as she backed away. She was beautiful with her creamy skin, short inky-colored straight hair, and clear blue eyes. She was petite in stature but possessed more than a handful of breast, a tiny waist and full, flaring hips, plus a nicely padded, very spank-able ass.

Talking soft, gentling her with his voice, he approached her. "Now, darlin', six smacks, that's all I'll be giving you for punishment this time. If I use my hand it'll be fifty, if it doesn't give out before then."

"Fifty!"

"Yes, your disobedience warrants it. I believe the paddle will be easier on you."

"Oh, I'm thinking a divorce might be the answer."

He sighed. "Are we going to go back down that road again? Besides, when this punishment session ends, I promise to introduce you to the play sessions you were interested in trying."

She bit her lip thoughtfully a moment, then sighed. "Okay." She started to return to the same position when he said, "Wait."

He took her arm and, without a word, with a firm look on his face, he placed her on all fours, her knees positioned near the foot of the bed, her calves, and ass hanging out over the edge. A perfect target, he decided as he enjoyed the view. Then he turned his mind back to the task at hand. "Stay like that, arms straight. Tilt your head back. It'll keep your back arched. Oh, you might want to close your eyes."

She gave him a confused look. "Why close my eyes and arch my back?"

"Arching the back makes your ass a better target, and closing your eyes might help you bear the pain."

Aaron saw her gulp then give an infinitesimal nod as she complied. He took up a position beside the bed, placed his left hand on her lower back. He drew the paddle back then came forward with an underhanded hit. The paddle landed against her plump ass with a satisfying *whack!* that reverberated through the silence of the room. The whack, while given with a medium strike flattened her ass at the same time lifting it up off the bed.

His wife's reaction seemed delayed for she stayed in position a few seconds then collapsed onto her stomach, wailing and clutching the spanked cheek.

Damn, he'd have to use an even lighter hand, it seemed.

"Oh, God, Aaron, I can't take this. I really can't," she sobbed.

Hardening his heart against the tears sliding down her cheeks, he said, "Five more, that's all. It'll be a bit easier on you I think if you lower your breasts, head, and shoulders to the bed. Leave your ass up high, though."

She sniffled as she slowly moved into the new position. "Okay. We'll try one more this way, if you think it'll be more tolerable. If it's not then I won't allow you to use that paddle on me, Aaron."

"You know, darling wife, you aren't the one to decide your punishment. That's my job."

With tears in her eyes, she tried changing his mind. "Aaron? I promise I won't ever drive again alone until you think I've had enough lessons."

He smiled. "You're right. After today's punishment, you'll remember in future not to drive, though tomorrow might be a good day to begin your driving lessons—assuming you can sit in the car."

"Very funny. Get on with it," she said between gritted teeth.

He saw the resolve on her face and felt proud of her. He moved slowly around to her backside, placed his hands on her hips, and readjusted her position. His gaze fell upon her ass then lower to her cunt, sweetly displayed. Then his gaze landed on her sweet rosy back door and he itched to reach out and finger that area, to shove his cock deep inside that dark, mysterious tight cavern. He wanted to give her pleasure, but then recalled the business at hand. Their love play would happen soon, he promised.

Aaron caught her glancing at him over her shoulder and, with a soft, knowing smile, she wiggled her ass at him. She was trying to entice him, the little tease!

He growled and gave her a hard swat with his hand. "Stay in position." He almost laughed aloud at her pouting expression until she turned away and lowered her breasts to the bed once more, brought her knees a bit forward, arching her back, her ass raised high.

Ah! The perfect position to deliver the just punishment she deserved he decided as he once again positioned himself at her side, his left hand spread over her lower back.

5

----

love my husband, I love my husband, the voice inside Jane said, over and over again as she awaited the rest of her punishment. There was no turning back now, besides, she truly needed this. She'd been a disobedient brat, much as her parents used to say to her. And, once he finished with her she had their play sessions to look forward to, wondering about that upcoming aspect of their marriage.

Kinky sex, that's what her sister would say, but wonderful, erotic, hot, wet sex was the description that came to Jane's mind. Jane felt ready to enter into a new realm, a new dimension in their marriage bed, longed for it. She felt a trickle down her inner thigh and gasped, realizing she was getting horny at her thoughts.

She heard Aaron say, "What have we here?" as he slid his finger from the apex of her thigh to the inside of her knee. "You naughty girl," he murmured silkily. "Feeling horny for your punishment, are you?"

"No!" Jane wailed. "Just thinking ahead to the play sessions."

"I was thinking along those lines too so let's get this over with."

She nodded and turned her head away from her husband, laying it on her pillow.

"Arch your back a bit more," Aaron ordered.

Jane brought her knees in closer to her body and heard Aaron say, "Perfect."

She cringed when she heard air move—twice—readying herself for the impact of wood against her butt again She thought she saw stars after the smack and groaned loudly at the unbelievable all encompassing pain radiating from her waist down to her thighs. She gasped but managed to stay in position.

"Good girl, here comes another," he warned. "And after this just three more."

She kept her hands folded under her head to keep from rubbing the stinging in her ass as he delivered another swift spank. As tears slid down her cheeks, she vowed she'd never give him reason to punish her this way. Never.

Then the paddle landed on the bed beside her and she looked at him over her shoulder. She rolled over and sat looking up at him. "You didn't finish."

"Yes, I did. It's enough. Never will I use that damned paddle on you, darling," he murmured as he took her in his arms and rubbed her sore bottom.

Aaron lay beside Jane, watching her sleep, stroking her sweat-dampened hair back from her forehead. He knew, when she wakened, she'd need to have a pain ointment rubbed into her ass, for it had turned a raw shade of red.

Never again would he use that paddle. Tomorrow he'd burn it in the fireplace. He thought about his reasons for using it on her in the first place and knew the true answer; he'd told her she would truly think hard about disobeying him again if he used the brutal paddle on her, which he knew was true. In the future, though, if he ever did have to discipline her again, he'd only use his hand.

Yet, now that he knew she was interested in pursuing a new erotic dimension of loving in their bedroom, including pleasurable spanking fun, it would be enough for him. Not that he'd *never* have to discipline her again, he knew he would, but he'd use his hand, or ruler, or possibly her hairbrush or the ping-pong paddles in the recreation room, but never anything harder than those items

When Jane wakened two hours later, it was past lunchtime and they were both hungry.

"I'll make us a sandwich and a cup of tomato soup," she said, easing off the bed. She lifted one leg and jammed it into her jeans but after the second leg, she couldn't pull the pants up over her rear. It was simply too painful. So she went to her closet and pulled on a long terry cloth robe.

"I'll make it. You rest," he said.

In the kitchen, she went to sit on the tall bar stool but as soon as one cheek touched the wooden seat she groaned in agony and eased down to the floor. "I'll make lunch," she said, "Since I can't sit anyway."

Guilt plagued Aaron. After lunch he said, "Come into our bedroom. I want to rub some ointment on you. It'll help with the swelling and pain."

In their bedroom, she laid down on the bed. Aaron raised her robe above her waist and paled at the condition of her ass. He liberally squeezed a pain-dulling ointment on his hands, rubbed them together a few times then started gently massaging the ointment over her buttocks.

As soon as his hands touched her, she reared up and shouted, "Do you have to do that so hard?"

He pressed her down and kissed the nape of her neck. She settled down and he murmured, "I barely touched you. I'm sorry, honey, but you've got two choices; endure the pain of allowing me to put the ointment on you and you'll feel some relief in a short while, or don't and be in pain all day long and probably tomorrow, too. Your choice."

"Do it," she said and gritted her teeth.

"Hold on a minute," he said as he rose from the bed. He returned with one of her long silk scarves, which he tied from one bedpost across to the other. "Grab hold of this and keep holding on while I do this. It'll help."

Jane held on for dear life, cringing as he tried to gently rub the ointment over every inch of her ass, paying particular attention to the areas of skin that were purpling just where her thighs and ass met. When he finished she laid her head on her pillow and said, "I'm going to sleep a little more, okay?"

He smiled. "I was going to suggest you do."

Aaron left her then and returned to the kitchen. Cleaning up their lunch debris, he then returned to the bedroom and found Jane sound asleep. He'd left her robe raised above her ass and the color of the skin hadn't changed at all. But he guessed she must be feeling some relief since she had fallen asleep. He picked up the frat paddle and carried it into the living room. There he lit a fire and was just putting the paddle into it when he stopped at the sound of his wife saying, "No! Aaron, stop. Don't do that."

He dropped it on the carpeted floor then rose and went to her. She wore the white terry robe yet and he carefully took her in his arms, keeping his hands well above her waist. "It's best I burn damned thing."

"I don't want you to," she whispered.

"Why not? I hate it," he spat.

"I'd like you to hang it behind the kitchen door on a hook. That way, whenever I'm thinking about doing something I shouldn't I'll see it there and will be reminded of what damage it can do."

"So, you want it as a visual reminder. You know I won't ever use it on you again, don't you?"

She nodded. "Yes, and I'm so glad you won't. Still, I need it as a reminder to help me, okay?"

"Okay," he said with a smile.

6

Three weeks later, Friday evening

Jane was nervous. Aaron would be home soon from a business trip. Any minute she expected him to rush into the house. She hadn't seen him in two weeks and, even though she hadn't misbehaved and there was nothing he would need to punish her for, she was still nervous.

Tonight was *the* night.

Tonight, after three weeks of waiting for her ass to heal, they'd be venturing into a new, spicier realm of making love with a 'play spank-sex session' as he called it. They'd both wanted this, had been looking forward to it, and now it would become a reality. They'd set the ground rules; each of them would voice what they liked to feel themselves, then what they wanted to try on the other. Each had the right to decline something but not until each made an attempt to try an idea first.

As Jane prepared a late, romantic supper, which they would eat once he arrived home, she tingled in anticipation of the things he would do to her body, and the things she would do to his. She felt moisture pooling in her vagina, leaking onto her panties. Damn, she would have to change them again since she could smell the lusty scent of her juices. But just then, Aaron drove up.

She raced into the living room just as he loped into the house. Dropping his suitcase on the floor, he strode to Jane and took her into his arms. Their wild kisses and joy at seeing each other led them to skipping supper and moving onto their pleasures.

Jane loved how her handsome husband always possessed a confident demeanor. He managed to master her, on several levels, and while she'd never refer to him or to anyone that he was her master and that he dominated her—he was—and he did. But it was private, between the two of him.

"You first," Jane whispered to him.

He grinned. "Glad you said that since I was going to insist I go first anyway."

She chided, "Ah, always the dominant."

Growling into the hollow of her neck, he said, "And you love it." He smacked her ass heartily.

Gasping, she leaned back and tried to escape his hold but he wouldn't release her. She grinned at him and asked, "What is your desire?"

Those were the words they decided they would use for this sexual play between them and now she could hardly believe, after weeks of anticipation that it was happening.

"I want to fuck you."

"You won't get any argument from me," she replied, giving him her siren's smile she'd practiced in a mirror while he'd been away.

"In the ass, in the kitchen, over the kitchen counter."

She readily slipped from his arms, sauntered into the kitchen. He followed and heard her say, "Hmm, I'll try the first, try mind you, since you know my feelings on the subject, but I'm not guaranteeing you any success. And I'm fine with the kitchen, or anywhere you like."

Leaning back casually against the kitchen counter, he said, "Oh, and one more desire; I want to fuck you after I've paddled your ass with that big white spatula."

Scowling, she said, "A spanking? Come on, Aaron!" she groaned.

"A spanking unlike anything you've ever received. Trust me. You'll love it."

She grumbled, "Okay," calling to mind Clarice's words regarding play spankings. "But remember that I'm still healing."

He just grinned. "I'll be careful. Now, come over here."

Obliging him, she moved to where he stood, facing the counter. She gasped in delight, and shivered after he moved behind her, cocooning her with his muscular arms and body. His left arm came around her waist and he pressed her down so her breasts lay flat on the counter. From a drawer at his elbow where he'd placed several sex toys, he pulled out a pair of velvet-lined handcuffs and proceeded to cuff her wrists to the handles of the drawers below.

She sighed. "You know, I never liked the idea that you bought these, Aaron. I won't back out if that's what you think so you don't need to cuff me."

"Heck, no, I know you won't, but captivity will give you a heightened sense of arousal. Trust me."

"Uh-huh, don't I always?"

"Smart ass," he said, unable to resist the delectable target. *Spank!*

She yelped then complained, "You promised not to do that so hard!"

"Sorry," he murmured. "Got carried away."

"Well, just remember I'm tied up here and can't defend myself."

"Yeah, every man's most erotic dream, having his favorite woman tied up. Now I want you to close your eyes and just... feel."

Jane did, trusting him completely. Shivers trailed up her spine when he walked his fingers up it. She wore a halter-top and he slowly untied it and pulled the top away from her body. Her bared breasts pressed against the counter "Aaron? Can you get a towel or something? This is uncomfortable."

"I'm getting something now," he said.

She saw him walk away from her, rummage in the bag he'd dropped on the kitchen floor upon entering the house. Her eyes widened on a contraption he pulled out of the bag.

It appeared to be a tube made out of black leather. Pausing beside her, he frowned. "I think I might have to remove the cuffs to get this on you."

"What in the world... " she started to ask, stunned when he held it up in front of her and pointed out what it was.

"See the holes? Your breasts poke out of it. It's a tube top with the best part of you bared.

"Oh, my, why it's the most ridiculous thing I've ever seen." She laughed and met his flinty-eyed look. "And this will turn you on?"

"Yes, even the thought of you wearing it turns me on."

She shrugged. "Unclamp the cuffs then."

He did and she struggled to pull it down her chest. He helped, settling it into place, his finger rimming the edges so her full breasts protruded out of it. He moved her over to a mirror in the hallway and said, "Aren't you something?" Grinning, he added, "You look fantastic." Standing behind her, he reached around her and rubbed the nipples until they formed stiff peaks and she groaned and ground her ass against him.

"Uh, uh," he said, dragging her back to the kitchen and over the counter where he cuffed her again. "I'm in control. This is my fantasy. Moving on...."

He found two medium-sized soft-edge bowls and pulled them from a drawer. He filled them with ice chips then cold water from the freezer and placed them on the countertop, guiding her nipples into them.

Jane gasped, "Aaron! This is painful."

"Not for long it won't be," he said. "In a few moments, your nipples will have numbed and you won't feel the cold any longer. Then I've another surprise for you."

"Oh, joy," she said, trying to sound enthusiastic. Right now, her focus was on her sore nipples. Within a minute, as he lounged against the counter watching her squirm in discomfort, her nipples lost all sensation. "Better," she said.

He clapped his hands. "Good, moving on... " He removed the cups of water. She watched him dip inside his pants pockets and remove two tiny metal objects. He opened the small clothespin clamps and closed them over her turgid nipples. She gasped in surprise at the sensations that travelled through her vagina. Her nipples were numb but the clamping of them produced just enough feeling to arouse her.

Jane narrowed her eyes on him when she realized he knew exactly what he was doing. The tension of the clips kept her nipples in an aroused state, and her clit throbbed continually, leaving her hanging and on the verge of orgasm, but not completion. God, she hated that feeling!

"Now, for the most important part," Aaron said with a wicked grin.

Standing behind her, he reached around her waist and unsnapped her white silky slacks and they slid to the floor. Her face heated up, knowing he was looking at her recent purchase, a surprise for him.

Stepping around to her side, he smiled into her face. "New underwear, hmm?"

Grinning, she said, "You like?"

"Oh, man, sweetheart, you are every man's fantasy."

"Glad to oblige," she replied, then wiggled her ass in the tiny panties emblazoned with a man's huge handprint and the words 'Spank Me' in the center.

"You do know I have to try them out, don't you?" he said.

She gave him a wicked little smile, dropped her head to the countertop and widened her legs, her feet still clad in silver stiletto heels, bracing herself for what she knew he'd do to her. "I knew you would want to."

"Is that a yes?" he asked.

"Yes," she said, hearing the hope in his voice she couldn't deny. "But no more than five and not too hard—please." She hated the pleading tone in her voice but knew she must give him warning since he had a tendency to get carried away where her ass was concerned.

"Thank you, sweetheart. I'm going to stand here by your side when I spank you. I want you to look only at my eyes. I want you to see what *you* do to me, giving yourself to me in this way, okay?"

She nodded and softly replied, "I understand, yes. I love you."

He kissed her forehead. "And I love you."

Standing at her side, she stared into his eyes even when she felt him move and knew he'd raised his hand. It smashed against her ass and she made a sound, "Oof," and expelled her breath with the first spank. She'd forgotten how large his hand was and how it covered so much of her ass. "Don't close your eyes against the impact. Just keep looking at me," he instructed.

She did, forcing herself to keep her eyes on him the entire time, though she wanted to close them against the smarting pain mixed with growing arousal when between spanks he rimmed her clitoris with his thumb.

*Spank-rim, spank-rim spank-rim, spank....*More than five she noted, counting, on the verge of orgasm, deciding she didn't want him to stop! But he did.

"Damn! Why'd you stop," she groaned. She felt her juices leaking from her body, sliding down her thighs, her clit tingling, waiting for more of the same.

She looked up then met the blatant sexual desire in his eyes. "I don't want you to come quite yet."

"Uh, Aaron?"

"Hmm?"

"How long is this fantasy of yours going to last, anyway?"

"Why do you want to know?"

She gasped when she felt him slowly pull down her panties.

"Cause I have equal time, you know."

"Your turn may have to wait until tomorrow. I'm not sure quite how long this will take. We didn't set any time limit, did we?"

"Wait just a minute, buddy, you can't do that!"

"Sure I can. I've got you cuffed. What are you going to do about it?"

"I'll scream!"

"Go ahead. I'll gag you."

She turned her head and met the laughter in his eyes. "You wouldn't dare."

A minute later Jane was cursing herself for opening her big mouth for he'd produced a two-inch ball gag, which he immediately strapped around her head. Pressing her lips together to avoid the ball he easily opened her mouth and jammed it into place. She tried to relax, resigned that she could do nothing about it.

"Ah, forgot something else."

Jane sighed, wondering what more could there be?

He dug inside another drawer and produced a little white, lace-trimmed apron. He tied it around her narrow waist and patted her ass, saying, "Perfect. Just how I like to see you dressed in the kitchen, serving me."

He meant 'servicing me', didn't he? she mused.

He was behind her again. She felt his body pressed close against her, then she jumped when she felt something wet and cold at the entrance to her ass. Moaning against the ball gag, she struggled frantically. He eased her panic when he said, "Don't worry, it's only some K-Y on my fingers I'm using—for now. You're so tight you need to be widened before I'll be able to enter you. This might take all night."

7

―――――――――

"*All night!*"

Jane started kicking back her heels again, hoping to connect with his legs, moaning loudly to get his attention. *No!* her mind screamed. He knew she didn't want to attempt it. How could he do this to her?

Aaron tried calming her. "Trust me, baby, you'll love this, once you get used to it. I promise not to hurt you, but only give you pleasure."

She calmed then until she felt him slide his finger deep inside her ass, then deeper still, adding a second finger beside it. It hurt! Yet, as he kept it inside her, she adjusted to it—actually enjoyed it—sort of... He removed his fingers and she sighed deeply in relief.

Her eyes widened then when she saw his arm come to her side and reach into the drawer beside her. He pulled out the big white plastic spatula and her moans increased. While she'd agreed to his fantasy—his desire to spank her with the spatula—she hadn't known at the time she'd be restrained. She hated the idea of not being able to move her body or speak.

"It's time for my fantasy to be fulfilled. Last time, you ready?"

She shook her head wildly.

Jane felt immediately guilty, caught the disappointment on his face as he started to unclasp one cuff. He stilled and looking from the cuff to her face, she nodded slowly, giving him permission to continue. She looked away from him and closed her eyes, waiting.

"Thank you, love," he said, and moved behind her again. "Just don't think too much, divorce yourself from your thoughts and just feel," he encouraged her.

Soon it wouldn't be just his fingers buried inside her sweet rosette between her lovely pink cheeks, he mused, growing aroused as he stared at her ass. Spreading a lubricant around her anus, dipping a digit inside her, widening her canal, he breathed deeply as he tried to control his growing lust. His one fantasy had always been taking his wife in the ass, hell, he'd never taken any woman that way, and it was a mysterious desire he wanted to fulfill. He wouldn't force Jane for he loved her, but he reasoned he'd be so gentle with her and he'd arouse her fully that she'd beg for him and accept him inside her body.

"One more thing, and this might be a little uncomfortable, but I promise, once you get used to it, you'll adore it, sweetheart."

He dug in the drawer again and found a butt plug, the smallest he'd purchased. He showed it to her and he saw her gulp, but waited for her permission. Finally, she nodded and turned away again.

"Thank you," he said humbly as he moved behind her again. He massaged her neck in an effort to relax her, stroked her from shoulder to ass, over and over again until he saw her visibly relax at his touch. "Here it comes," he said. "Take a deep breath and hold it, think about opening yourself to me—relax your ass, and it'll slide right in," he encouraged her. "I'm using the smallest plug for today, then we'll move onto a larger one tomorrow. Hopefully, by tomorrow night, you'll be able to take me inside you."

He paused putting in the plug when he saw she'd jammed her legs together. Knowing it to be an unconscious act to protect her bottom he smiled and put the plug down on the counter. He kneeled behind her, slid his hand between her thighs, stroked up her thigh until he reached the apex. There he pressed his thumb directly on her clitoris, stroked it, rubbed it in circles until she groaned and wiggled her ass from side to side. Oh, yeah, she was aroused he noticed as her juices slickened his thumb. He slid a finger inside her cunt, pulled it out, then rimmed the outside of her clitoris, ending by tapping it with his index finger. She groaned louder and opened her legs wide.

Aaron loved looking at her legs in the stilettos, his gaze moving from the shoes up her firm calves to her muscular thighs smiling at the twin globes of her fine ass above. He realized he'd never seen her body from this view before, and loved it. His gaze dropped below her ass to her cleft between her thighs, the tip of her clit peeking out.

Time to give her a reward he decided and reaching up with his thumbs he spread her lips, revealing her clitoris. It was small and pink. He wanted it to grow for him, turn red for him, throb for him so he proceeded to tongue her sweet little bud over and over until it did grow—twice as big—and it turned as red as a cherry. No throbbing yet but soon he knew it would, especially after he suckled it between his teeth, nibbled then blew on it.

He'd done that to her only once before—when she'd drunk too much wine and lost all of her inhibitions a few months ago. Tonight, without any booze, because they'd made commitments to each other, he knew she'd cooperate fully with anything he wanted to do to her body.

Jane wriggled her ass faster, in time with his tongue that stabbed, stroked, and rimmed her clit until she stiffened, gave a muffled scream behind the gag and jerked her hips in time with her orgasm.

When she stopped moving, Aaron rose behind her and whispered, "Now wasn't that nice?"

She nodded, looked at him gratefully, her eyes telling him he'd satiated her and she loved him for it.

He said, "That was for you, what's next is for me."

He liked how her eyes widened when he picked up the butt plug once more. She watched him smear a lubricant all over the tip then moved behind her where he couldn't see her face any longer and she couldn't see his. He positioned the small plug at the entrance of her sweet rosette, pressed the rounded tip inside a bit. Her entire body stiffened including her ass. He frowned, smartly slapped each cheek and said, "No tightening up. Keep loose, sweetheart and you'll easily be able to take it."

Aaron was relieved when she did relax, from her spine through her ass cheeks and, while fingering her clit again with the fingers on his left hand, he slowly pressed the plug in further with the right. He had to smack her ass again, encouraging her to loosen her spinchter muscle. With just a few more gentle pushes, he was able to push the plug in and past the flared center, fashioned to hold it in place, seating it deep inside her. The end of the plug was capped with a yellow daisy and he grinned when he looked down on her rosy hole decorated with the flower.

"You look beautiful, Jane," he murmured. "Would you like to see it?"

Her eyes widened on him and she shook her head.

"Yes, you do need to see this and see how happy this makes me."

Aaron left the kitchen and found her big round magnified hand mirror in the bathroom. He angled it in front of her face so she could catch the reflection of her butt-plugged ass in a mirror hanging on the wall over the sink.

Again, she widened her eyes on her ass decorated prettily with a daisy then met his eyes. He caught the desire in her gaze and he felt his cock grow. He put the mirror down and leaning over her, he trailed kisses from her neck and down her spine, ending at the daisy. Then he moved to each side, gently biting her ass cheeks. From her little squeals behind the ball gag and the way she was dancing her ass around in circles, he knew she liked what he was doing to her. He reached for the spatula, gripped the handle, drew his hand back and lightly smacked her.

She tensed up when she saw the spatula in his hand.

"Stay loose. I'm only going to give you pleasure with this, darlin'."

And he did, spanking her all over her creamy-colored ass, turning it a pale, delightful pink down to her upper thighs, varying the spanks, some light, some harder, but never the spanking he'd given her when he'd disciplined her. This was spanking meant for pure pleasure. Then he turned the spatula sideways and slid it between her legs, rubbing her clitoris until she screamed out her pleasure once more behind the ball gag, her body shattering with her orgasm.

He started in again with the same treatment until she came twice more, her womanly juices sliding down her legs. He dropped the spatula on the floor, unzipped his jeans, and pulled his cock out of his briefs, positioning himself behind her. He heard her shrieking behind gag, knowing if she weren't gagged, she'd be shouting out her pleasure. Then he slowly, torturously (for him) slid inside her cunt then proceeded to ride her fast and hard, as though riding a horse, slapping her ass and thighs with one hand, keeping close contact with her clitoris with the other, knowing he could give her pleasure again in this position.

Aaron held himself back, riding her for a long while, feeling when she came, contracting her vagina around his cock. Finally, he couldn't hold himself back any longer and he spewed his cum inside her, stayed locked inside her until his climax dissipated. Even afterwards, he was hard, still aroused so he stayed inside her, reached beneath her and fingered her until she climaxed again. As he slowly left her body, he saw she was exhausted for she'd slumped on the kitchen counter.

His pretty wife would sleep well tonight.

After releasing her from the handcuffs, he lifted her into his arms and carried her to their bed. Already, he saw, she' fallen asleep. Gently he pulled off the ball gag, pulled off the nipple clips and, after turning her over to her stomach, reached for the butt plug but then recalled his decision to penetrate her anally soon. Besides, he enjoyed the sight of it there, knowing it would be doing its job while she slept. He tucked her in, undressed and crawled in beside her.

A aron wakened Saturday morning glad he didn't have to rise and go to work. He frowned though with his eyes closed, feeling something on his wrists and ankles. He raised his head and through sleepy eyes, noticed Jane wasn't beside him in bed. He also realized he was lying prone, on his stomach with his arms and legs spread-eagled and cuffed to the four bedposts, naked except for his briefs which he'd worn to bed.

He sighed. She was at it already. Taking her turn with him. Grinning, he wondered what she planned—until he saw her reflection in the big mirror on the wall, as she entered. She wore black thigh high boots. Lifting his gaze and straining his neck, he gulped when he saw her dressed in a tiny red thong and red corset that she'd laced tight, her waist small enough he knew he could span it with his hands. The top of her breasts were plump and overflowed the corset. She wore a pretty black velvet choker around her neck and her short hair had been brushed to lay close against her head.

"Good morning, Sunshine," she said sweetly, smiling at him in the mirror as she sauntered nearer. "Wake up, honey, it's my turn," she purred.

Aaron's eyes widened when she pulled a small single thronged whip from behind her back and snapped it over his prone body. He gasped when the tip flicked across his ass causing a hot searing pain. Looking into the mirror at the satisfied look on her face, he said, "You're telling me this is your idea of a fantasy?"

She nodded. "Right on, honey." With a snap of her wrist she flicked it once more, the whip licking his left ass cheek and hip and leaving a stinging pain behind.

He gritted his teeth, refusing to voice his pain. Then he said, "I thought you accepted my being the dominant partner in our marriage?"

She grinned like a shark. "I do, but remember, this is love play—my little secret—my little fantasy. Surprised, huh?"

"I'll say," he said, noticing the small kitchen knife in her hand. He started pulling against the cuffs. Wielding the knife efficiently she slit his briefs on either side and pulled them off him. He closed his eyes against the sight of her reflection in the mirror as she focused on his ass. Damn, he was beginning to see how vulnerable she'd felt!

8

S oon he found himself shouting in both pain and pleasure from each flick of the whip. After she'd whipped him several times she dropped the whip and he groaned with relief, his ass feeling as if she'd lighted a fire on it. Then he gulped when he saw her reach up to the top of her dresser and pull down what appeared to be a leather-clad ping-pong paddle only several inches larger in circumference.

"Damn it, Jane, that's enough!" he roared, wondering where the paddle came from.

She answered his silent question, saying, "You think you're the only one who paid a visit to that little sex shop downtown?" She frowned and paused beside him, standing in what he'd call a dominatrix position, a hand on one hip, one hand holding the paddle, limbs spread wide. Lord but his cock throbbed against the mattress, thinking how he'd never thought she looked more sexy—or more dangerous.

"Come on, honey, you said you'd honor my fantasy after I honored yours. Don't you trust me?"

Put like that he immediately felt guilty. He nodded. "I do trust you, but, well…"

"I know," she said, giving him a devilish grin, "You're not in charge. That's what's bothering you, isn't it?"

He nodded, straining his neck as he kept his eyes focused on her.

She shrugged. "Too bad. You're not in a position to do anything about it, are you? Ride it out, honey, this is my fantasy. You can still be the disciplinary boss, though, in our household. I promise."

"Damned right I am. You'll pay for this, you know," he warned.

She grinned. "I'm counting on it."

Good grief! His wife was kinkier than he ever imagined she'd be and his cock throbbed painfully beneath him. He loved this side of her, yet hated it too.

She moved into position beside him. In the mirror, he saw her raise her arm high then down as the paddle crashed against his ass.

He cursed under his breath, his gaze never leaving her reflection in the mirror as she delivered the next several slaps, alternating in an even cadence against each cheek. Soon a chill arose over his entire body, from head to toe, and his cock throbbed against the mattress furiously. She'd lightened her slaps and while they stung, they weren't so painful enough that he couldn't tolerate them. He had to admit he was aroused, and soon he was so close to orgasm he begged her to slap him harder. She obliged him and then he came, spewing his cum against the mattress, wishing he were inside her sweet cunt.

Afterwards, breathing heavily, he lifted his head and met her gaze in the mirror. Softly, she said, "My desire. My fantasy. You like it, don't you?"

Slowly he nodded, then fell into a deep, welcomed slumber. She'd quite literally exhausted him. He wakened some time later with a start when he felt her hands releasing his ankles. Looking up into the mirror again, he saw she sat behind him on the bed, still dressed in her enticing red outfit. Then he noticed the tube of K-Y jelly in her hand and grimaced at her plans for him.

"No way, Jane," he said firmly, "I'm drawing the line here…"

"What? It's okay for you to stick a butt plug up my ass so you can have anal sex with me in the future but not suffer the same treatment?"

"Suffer?" he scoffed. "You enjoyed it. Admit it."

"I admit I was afraid at first, but now, though I think it's fair to give you the same—joy. No need to worry. I'm not going to have anal sex with you with a dildo if that's what you're worried about."

He breathed a sigh of relief. "What then?" he asked.

"I thought I'd give you an extra thrill and massage your prostate, that's all."

Aaron knew about this, having heard plenty about the tricks whores sometimes performed on the married men at the club when they couldn't get their wives to participate in such unusual sex acts.

"Do your worst, lady," he said. "Your time will come."

Laughing, she said, "On your knees, husband. I can't penetrate you in this position."

Groaning, yet excitement flaring through him at her words, he got up on his knees then playfully wagged his ass at her. She smacked him smartly and he gasped.

"Hold still," she ordered.

He did, startled when she smeared the cold jelly around his small, rosy hole. He was shivering—in anticipation of feelings he imagined he'd never felt before. Watching her slip on a latex glove, he couldn't control his body's response as he imagined her entering his body. His cock hardened then curled up against his stomach.

"Shit, Jane!" he yelped when she reached beneath him and wound her fingers around his cock and pumped him with a hard, quick motion.

Damn!" he shouted, climaxing almost immediately. He collapsed on the bed and he shivered when she leaned over him, felt her short hair brush his neck.

"How was that? Surprised you, didn't I?"

"I'll say," he whispered.

Playfully, lightly, she slapped his ass again with the leather paddle. "Get back into position," she ordered and he scrambled to get up onto his knees.

Cold hit his anus and he groaned when she slipped her fingers just inside his anal canal and pressed lightly on his prostate. Her fingers were small and she eased them in a short distance, the entry much easier than when he'd penetrated her with the plug, he realized. Her fingers waggled inside him, massaging him, his arousal building quickly. The gentle massage made his cock harden again. The little witch knew when he was close to coming and backed off, easing her fingers out of him, leaving him sweating and needy. Oh, she deserved to be punished, her ass blistered for this treatment. At the same time, he thought he'd kiss her feet and ass if she gave him the treatment again.

Finally, after several massages, she allowed him release and he exploded, his cum spewing across the sheets. Sweating profusely, he begged her, "Please, Jane. I need to lie down. And could you release the handcuffs?"

"Go ahead," she said softly, patting his buttocks as she moved from the bed. Leaning over him, she released his wrists.

With his head lying on his pillow, he watched her put the paddle away, and the cuffs. Suddenly, exhaustion left him and he whispered, "You didn't take out the plug, did you?"

Grinning wickedly at him over her shoulder, she asked, "What would you do if I did?"

"I'd have to beat your ass until you begged me to stop, or begged me to give you more," he growled.

"It's still there," she said. "Wanna see?"

He gulped, nodded, and watched her bend over, ease her fingers into the sides of her thong and pull down the tiny triangular piece of red satin. There sat the golden daisy, waiting to be replaced by the larger plug with a big red rose on the end, then, finally, her ass would be ready to accept his big cock buried deep inside her as he rode her to fulfillment he could only imagine.

Life with Jane would never be boring.

THE END

THANK YOU FOR READING

Did you enjoy this book?

We invite you to leave a review at the website of your choice, such as Goodreads, Amazon, Barnes & Noble, etc.

DID YOU KNOW THAT LEAVING A REVIEW...

- Helps other readers find books they may enjoy.
- Gives you a chance to let your voice be heard.
- Gives authors recognition for their hard work.
- Doesn't have to be long. A sentence or two about why you liked the book will do.

Don't miss out on your next favorite book!

Join the Melange Books mailing list at
www.melange-books.com/mail.html

Subscriber Perks Include:

- First peeks at upcoming releases.
- Exclusive giveaways.
- News of book sales and freebies right in your inbox.
- And more!

ABOUT NANCY PIRRI

Nancy Pirri started writing several years ago while raising four children. Nancy has been a member of Romance Writers of America and her local chapter, Midwest Fiction Writers, for nine years. She is also one of the founders of a second Minnesota RWA chapter, Northern Lights Writers (NLW).

www.nancypirri.com

ABOUT TARA FOX HALL

Tara Fox Hall's writing credits include nonfiction, horror, suspense, action-adventure, erotica, and contemporary and historical paranormal romance. She is the author of the paranormal action-adventure *Lash* series and the vampire romantic suspense *Promise Me* series. Tara divides her free time unequally between writing novels and short stories, chainsawing firewood, caring for stray animals, sewing cat and dog beds for donation to animal shelters, and target practice.

www.tarafoxhall.com

Eye of the Storm

Tempest of Vengeance

Sundown & Serena

Hope's Return

Fate's Prison

Web of Memory

Forever

Freedom: Elle's Story

Novellas

Return To Me

Surrender to Me

The Oath

Anthologies

The Origin of Fear in Spellbound 2011 Anthology

Night Music in Midnight Thirsts II Anthology

Partners in Midnight Thirsts II Anthology

Kink in Wicked Christmas Wishes Anthology

The Oath in Wicked Christmas Wishes Anthology

Make Me Behave Anthology

Latham's Landing, An Anthology